THE FIRE TRILOGY

Thief's Fire

J.L. HACKETT

Cover art by Havock Satterly

ISBN-13: 978-0615939438 (HP&SG Publishing)

ISBN-10: 0615939430

Acknowledgements

I'd like to acknowledge my bestest friend ever, Rachel, for helping me edit my book. My friend, Jasmine, for helping with the editing as well.

I'd like to also thank my awesome cousin Magen for helping with the finishing editing of my book. You're amazing and I love you!

To my best friend, Sara, for pushing me to write and publish my work as well as designing my book covers.

Prologue

It was a time of war and destruction. A time when darkness ruled the hearts of many. A time when a group called the Elementals ruled. This group was born Human, but at fifteen when they came of age a power was awakened inside of them, powers of fire, water, earth, or air. When the Elementals first came into existence, they were seen as protectors of the Human race, the mediators of power between the Humans and the other magical beings that lived in our world. Without them, the Fae and Witches would declare war on one another and the Humans would be the ones to pay the highest price, for they were the only ones not gifted with magical abilities.

As the years went by and generation after generation of Elementals were born, the power that was supposed to be used to protect turned into one of pure destruction. They saw themselves as gods instead of gifted Humans. They used their abilities to force not only the Humans they had sworn to protect to worship them but also the Witches and Fae. Finally, their destruction and power became too much for the three groups to bear. Witches, Fae, and Humans banded together to fight against the Elementals, to end their reign and destroy them forever.

One by one, the families were destroyed, the gifts of the Elementals dying with them until only one Elemental, a child, remained. This Elemental had been taken in by a rogue Witch. The Witch knew that it was only a matter of time before he and the child were found. As he looked at the girl, a pain shot through him. This was a baby, not a killer. He had taken her in and raised her as his own. He knew that no matter what he couldn't let anything happen to her. One night he sensed that their time was coming to a close. As the Witch looked at the child, a smile spread across his face. This one would not be like the others. She would be strong and pure. He knew that she would not help destroy or conquer.

As he looked at her he knew that there was only one thing he could do for her. He couldn't save himself, but he could save this girl from the destruction and hatred that was, at that moment, surrounding them. He knew that if he did this his powers would be depleted and he would die, but he also knew that he had no choice. As he looked at the child, he knew that she was the Elemental of the prophecy. He knew that the prophecy must come to pass. If not, then their world would never have peace again. Never would they step out of the darkness and into the light that was once their beautiful world. The Witch closed his eyes and with all the power that was within him, he gave his life for the greater good. He said his last incantation as their house was consumed by flames.

Chapter One

A cloaked woman stood in the middle of the room, her face covered by a scarf and hood. "Our spy tells us that the documents are located in a Witch's house in the small town near Thief's Cave. We," the man said as he looked around the room at the other council members, "want you and your partner to retrieve the papers at all cost. We can't have that information falling into Damian's hands. He is growing more powerful by the day. It will only be a matter of time before our secret is found out, but we will try to conceal it from him a little longer." The Council looked down at the woman and nodded their agreement. "Go, and be careful."

The woman nodded her head and left the room.

~~~

Falon sat with her back to the far wall and scanned the bar. For what seemed like the hundredth time in mere minutes, she tied her hair back at the nape of her neck. She sighed in frustration as a piece of hair immediately worked its way out of the tie. "Come on, Ariana," she said under her breath as she waited for her friend to show up. They had a job to do and she really wanted to get it over with. Falon scanned the room again and a small smile played at the corner of her lips as a blond-haired woman came walking towards her. "It's about time," she said as she used her foot to shove a chair towards her friend.

"Sorry, I'm running a tad late," Ariana said as she looked at her friend. She frowned when she saw the dark circles under Falon's eyes. Ariana shook her head as she took in Falon's disheveled appearance. Her red hair was pulled back like normal, but her clothes and eyes said that she had been on a long journey. "You haven't been sleeping well?"

"No," Falon said as she rubbed her face with her hands. "Listen, how about we get some food in us, go do this job, then go home for a while."

Ariana gave her friend a small smile. "That sounds nice," she said as she waved over the barkeeper. He smiled at them as he came over. "Hello, James."

"Red," he said, nodding towards Falon, "Goldy." The girls smiled as they looked at the man. They had known him for about three years now and every time they came in here he called them Red and Goldy. "So, the usual?"

"That would do nicely," Ariana said being her charming self. She looked back at Falon. "How was the council meeting?"

Falon looked at James and nodded so that he would leave. "It went," she said as she rubbed the back of her neck. "We are to steal the documents back at all cost."

"Yes, I know," Ariana said as she gave Falon a cocky smile.

"If you knew, why did you ask?" Falon asked with a smirk.

"Conversation." She looked over at Falon and noticed that her friend had grown stiff. Ariana watched as Falon pulled the hood of her cloak up and covered her face with a scarf so that only her brown eyes were visible. Ariana looked into her friend's eyes and knew that trouble was brewing. She slowly pulled her hood up as well, hiding her from whatever enemy Falon was seeing. "What is the trouble, my friend?" she asked, not turning to look at what had caught Falon's attention.

"Fae Bounty Hunters," Falon said as she looked around the room for an escape. She knew that the odds of the Bounty Hunters being there for them weren't good, but she didn't want to take a chance. Not with them being this close to their prize. "We must leave," she said as she touched Ariana's hand.

At Falon's touch, Ariana was pulled into a vision--a vision that took her breath away. "We can't," Ariana said desperately.

"Don't do this, Ariana. Don't," Falon said, pointing her finger in Ariana's face. She sighed as she saw the stubborn set of her friend's jaw. There would be no talking Ariana out of whatever had entered her head.

"We must stay," Ariana said with a worried expression. "We must save them."

Falon looked at her friend in shock. "No! Absolutely not. I won't risk my neck and our *job* for some Fae bounty hunters." Falon crossed her arms in front of her chest and stared Ariana down.

"They are very important to the future. *Our* future. We must help them." Ariana glanced over her shoulder and saw the two tall men that had Falon's attention. If her vision was correct, they had very little time before those two ended up dead. "Falon, trust me."

Falon rubbed her face with her hand and sighed deeply. "Of all the Witches for me to make friends with, it had to be you, a bloody seer." Falon looked at Ariana and gave her a small smile. "I do trust you. What do I need to do?"

"You take the dark-haired Fae and knock him to the ground. If you don't, then that Witch over in the corner is going to kill him," Ariana said jerking her head towards the Witch that Falon had noticed earlier. She knew by the way he and his three friends looked that they were up to no good.

"Right, now just so we get this straight, we are going to interfere in a Witch and Fae dispute that will put us in the middle."

Ariana nodded but said nothing.

Falon pinched the bridge of her nose. "You are going to get me killed by the end of the night."

"No, it is not your time. Everything will be fine," Ariana said with a smile.

"Why do I not find that comforting? Oh I remember. Because your visions have a habit of not being completely clear. Bloody seer," Falon said, glaring at her friend. She then looked at the two men. "Ariana, they both have dark hair," she said, her voice rising in annoyance. How was she supposed to know which one to save if they both had dark hair?

"The one with the longer dark hair. I believe his Fae mark is red. The others is silver," Ariana said as she looked at the tattoos on the side of the men's necks. Every Fae was born with a mark on their necks so that everyone else knew what they were, just like every Witch was born with silver or gold eyes.

"Great. I get the mean-looking one. You know this is probably going to end badly?" Falon said. Every time Ariana had a vision she ended up injured in some way. She was really not looking forward to this.

"Stop being so negative," Ariana said. "Just get ready. I promise these two are really important."

"Very well. I'm trusting you my friend, but if it comes down to us or them, I choose us." Falon then prepared to move when Ariana signaled.

~ ~ ~

As Aidan entered the bar, his green eyes scanned the crowd. He and Cale had been hunting a Witch and they had finally cornered him. "This is a bad idea, Aidan," Cale said as he looked around the room.

"We are just going to get him and get out," Aidan said, his voice calm and sure as always.

"Yeah, and the fact that we are in a Witch town, in a Witch bar is not going to be a problem," he said sarcastically. "This is a suicide mission my friend," Cale said, looking over at his best friend and leader.

"That is a mere technicality, not a problem and this is not a suicide mission." Aidan looked at Cale. "Have you lost your nerve for this job already?" he asked with a raised eyebrow and a scoff. "Maybe you should wait outside."

Cale growled at him through clenched teeth. "Don't push my patience. Besides, I'm not the one that looks like the walking dead. When was the last time you got a good night's sleep?"

"I can't seem to get the dreams to lessen. I have always had them, but lately they have gotten stronger." Aidan closed his eyes as he thought about the beautiful voice and presence that haunted his dreams. He never saw the woman's face, but he felt her. She was a beautiful lie to believe in. Aidan knew that she wasn't real, that he would never meet her, but it was still nice to think about her.

"Maybe you are getting close to meeting her. You are old. Most Fae have met their mates by your age," Cale said jokingly.

"No, my mate died years ago. This is just Fate's way of torturing me." Aidan gave him a ghost of a smile then scanned the room again. He needed to get focused and get his mind off of the woman that had haunted him for a thousand years. The woman he would never know. Aidan's small smile faded as he saw two hooded figures in the corner. It was never a good sign for someone to not want to be seen. After this job he would have to figure out who the two were. As Aidan was turning his head back towards the other people in the bar, his eyes caught the Witch they were after. As he stared him down, the man's face grew smug and it was then that Aidan realized that Cale had been right. This was a suicide mission. Man, he really needed to get some sleep if he was making foolish mistakes like this.

~ ~ ~

Falon closely watched the Fae she was supposed to help and even from this distance she could see how attractive he was. He had black hair that came to his shoulders, beautiful green eyes, and a red Fae mark on his neck. He was also taller then the Fae next to him. She shook her head to get focused. Something about this Fae was different. It was as if she was being drawn to him, like Fate was pulling them together, twisting their lives by just being in the same room. Falon's eyes narrowed as she thought about Fate. Fate was stupid.

Falon waited until the last possible moment to act. She hurried over to the Fae and knocked him to the ground, feeling the bolt that the Witch had sent fly over her head. The heat of the blast penetrated her cloak. That was really close. *Too* close.

Aidan was stunned by the hooded figure knocking him to the floor. Before he could think, his body acted, instincts taking over and he pushed the stranger away, slashing at him with his knife.

Falon felt the knife slice across her side as the Fae fought against her. She rolled away enough to avoid getting cut a second time. This is what she got for doing what Ariana asked her to do. She felt the blood begin to run down her body. That was definitely going to leave a mark.

Aidan was about to attack again when he felt the heat from the blast coming from behind him. He looked over his shoulder and stood there for a moment in shock as he saw the hole in the wall behind where he had been standing. If the hooded figure hadn't of knocked him down, he would be dead right now. How could his senses have been that off? Not only had he not been prepared for an attack, but he had also hurt the person who had saved him. Suddenly, all the anger that Aidan had been feeling turned to guilt as he looked down and saw the blood on the blade of his knife.

Falon saw the realization of the situation dawn in the Fae's eyes. Good, the stupid idiot finally realized she was a good guy. She shook her head to clear it from the pain that was coursing through her side and slowly stood up. Falon looked around for Ariana, hoping that she was having a better time than she was. As her eyes fell on Ariana and the other Fae she saw a look on his face that was very odd. She was confused by the look of shock and awe that was there. Falon shook her head, not understanding what all that was about and really not caring. All she wanted to do was get her friend out of there and let these Fae handle their own problems. Falon looked around the room to find the Witches that were causing so much trouble. Panic filled her as she saw a Witch aiming at Ariana and the other Fae, preparing to fire another bolt. Falon was trying to get her feet moving so that she could help her friend, but in her mind she knew that she was too far away to help. As she watched, the Fae rolled Ariana to her back and covered her with a shield ultimately protecting her from danger. Falon was about to handle the Witch when she was suddenly on her stomach, the force of the fall knocking the breath out of her.

"Stay down!" Aidan yelled as the Witch sent another burst of power at them.

This is really getting old, Falon thought as her mind cleared from the pain and her breathing went back to normal.

Aidan put up a shield around him and the hooded figure as the Witch sent a third blast of power at them. The stupid Human under him tried to move again. "I said stay down," he said through gritted teeth. What was this guy's problem? Did he want to get himself killed?

"I heard you the first time," Falon said as she moved her hand under her cloak to the bag that was draped across her shoulder. Once her hand found the device she was looking for, she brought it out and slid it across the floor so that it was at the feet of the Witch who were attacking them. Falon said the incantation to get the device to work and smiled as the Witch looked down in shock. The device exploded, knocking him unconscious. "Please get off of me," she said as she spoke to the man that was still on top of her.

Aidan was shocked when a woman's voice came out from under the hood, and when he looked over his shoulder and saw the Witch unconscious. He thought that she was just a human, but now he wasn't quite certain. Aidan quickly got off the girl, then jerked her around until she was looking at him.

There was no way that it was a woman, he thought. He couldn't have been saved by a mere woman, especially a human. Aidan frowned and jerked down the scarf that covered the woman's face. His breath caught in his throat as he stared down at a beautiful woman. As he looked into her eyes and saw the brown color to them he knew for sure that this woman was a human. Great, a human woman had saved him. How embarrassing.

"You're a woman," Aidan said incredulously.

"You are very perceptive," Falon said sarcastically as she pushed him away from her. As she turned around, she was faced with two more Witches. "Really? Do you two not have anything better to do?" This was getting ridiculous. All she had wanted when she entered the bar tonight was to get a good meal then head to work. Instead, she was bleeding, in pain, and about to face off with two more Witches. Why she couldn't have a friend who didn't see the future, she would never know. She would blame Fate yet again for making her life more complicated.

Aidan stood next to the woman and tried to shove her behind him. "Are you insane?" he asked as he looked around the room. Not only were there two more Witches in front of them, but Cale had two in front of him and the other woman. Aidan frowned as he realized that Cale's savior had been a woman as well. He looked over his shoulder to get a better look at his savior, but most of her was still concealed by her cloak and hood. Why couldn't her hood of fallen down like the other woman's?

"I'm not insane, nor am I the one not paying attention," Falon said as she noticed that the Fae was looking at her instead of the

Witches who were sneering at them. "Move!" she yelled, shoving the Fae. As she pushed him away she grabbed two more devices out of her bag and threw one at the Witches coming towards them and the other at the ones that were about to attack Ariana and the other Fae. After a quick incantation, the devices released a gas that made the men fall to the ground unconscious. Once the Witches were out, Falon looked over at Ariana and scoffed when she saw that she'd been shoved behind the Fae's back. "Your friend should have let my friend handle the problem. Then I wouldn't have had to interfere," Falon said with a little bit of annoyance.

"He was just protecting her. Most Humans need protection," Aidan said as he looked down at the woman.

"She's a Witch, not a Human, and we don't need help. Nor do we want it," Falon said as she glared at the Fae.

Aidan shook his head then they both walked over to Cale and Ariana. Falon pulled Ariana to the side, away from the two Fae. "We must go. Now."

Ariana looked at Falon with a sadness in her eyes that Falon had never seen. "Don't. Whatever it is, just don't. We have a job to do," Falon said through clenched teeth as she tried to push the pain in her side away. Her side was really hurting and it was all because of that...that *Fae.*

"I can't leave him," Ariana said as she looked over her shoulder and saw the two Fae talking. "He's my mate." She sounded weak and helpless. "Please, Falon. Please."

Falon rubbed her temples with her fingers. "Ariana, we don't have time for this." She then looked up and her eyes met her friend's eyes. She sighed deeply as she saw the hurt in them. "Fine. When we finish our job we will find them, but we have to leave right now."

Ariana's shoulders sagged. "But what if we can't find them?"

Falon glared at Ariana, "Have I ever said something that I did not mean? Have I *ever* broken a promise to you?" she asked as she grabbed Ariana's shoulders so that she was looking straight at her.

"No," Ariana said with a pout.

"Then trust me, I promise we will find him. Now, come on," Falon said as she headed out of the bar. She smirked as they slipped past the Fae unnoticed. Those two were some of the most unobservant Fae bounty hunters she had ever seen. Falon shook her head, and vowed to put the Fae out of it. She had a job to do and she needed to be focused.

~ ~ ~

"We need to go," Aidan said to Cale as he tried to keep his eyes off the two women talking a few feet away. He was especially interested in the one who had saved him. Why he was feeling drawn to her he didn't know. So far she had shown that she was stubborn, sarcastic, and annoying. She was definitely not the type of woman he liked to be around. So why was he being drawn to her? Aidan shook his head and tried to focus on what his friend was saying.

"I can't leave her, Aidan," Cale said with a desperation in his voice that neither of them had ever heard before. He knew that Aidan would see it as a weakness, but he didn't care. The very idea of leaving his mate made his heart quicken and his chest tighten. He couldn't believe that he had finally found her. Cale closed his eyes in frustration, not at the fact that he had found his mate, but because she was a Witch. Why couldn't she have been a Fae? Cale shook his head. It didn't matter. She was his mate and no matter what, she was his.

"We aren't taking them with us. We have enough to worry about without worrying about two women. What has gotten into you?" Aidan asked. It was not like Cale to be this emotional about something. Cale was a joker, but he was not one to get upset or frantic. It was just odd.

"She's my mate, Aidan. I won't leave her," Cale said as he grabbed Aidan's arms and shook him. Aidan was taken back by the fierceness of Cale's voice. Cale quickly let go of him and ran his hand through his short brown hair. "Listen, I know it's crazy, but I can't leave her."

"Cale, she is a Witch," Aidan said with a sound of disgust. It wasn't as if he didn't like Witches, but it was not very often that the groups joined together. It was even rarer for a Fae and Witch to be mates. Aidan shook his head at how this night had gone completely crazy. *Fate*, Aidan thought with a scoff.

24

"I know she is a Witch, but it doesn't change the fact that she is my mate. Aidan, I have been waiting for her, and I can't lose her now that I've found her. For some reason Fate has decided that I'm meant to be with a Witch so I'll deal with that, but I won't lose her," Cale said as he looked at his friend.

Aidan pinched the bridge of his nose as he contemplated all the things that could and probably would go wrong with bringing those women with them. "Fine, but you're responsible for them. If they cause problems or get into trouble it is on you, not me. Is that clear?"

Cale's face broke out in a huge smile. "Very." He turned around quickly. Aidan followed his friend's example and looked around the bar. He guessed he was going to have to be sociable if the women were going to be with them all the time now. Great, he was going to get to spend more time with Little Miss Sarcastic. As Aidan focused on his surroundings he noticed that the women were gone. He watched as Cale hurried outside. Aidan followed after him and as he came out into the night he realized that the women were no where in sight.

"Where did they go?!" Cale asked, his voice panicked.

Aidan sighed deeply. "I don't know, but we will find them," he said as he placed his hand on his friend's shoulder. He knew that Cale had always kept himself open for his mate which made finding her easier, but it also made him more sensitive about her. Aidan had always kept himself closed off, protected, especially after finding out that he would never know his mate. After that, he just didn't keep himself open to anything or anyone. What was the point? Aidan had learned long ago that you never lose control of your emotions and you definitely never let them control you. He shook his head then shoved Cale down the alley. "Let's go find your mate and Miss Sarcastic."

Chapter Two

"You promise we will find him?" Ariana asked, for what seemed like the hundredth time in an hour, as they walked in the shadows of the buildings.

"Yes. I believe I have already said that, unless you were thinking I was going to change my mind since the last time you asked me. Which was when? Oh yes, three minutes ago," Falon said, frustrated with this whole thing. "Stupid man. Side bleeding. Always getting hurt because of her visions. Doesn't believe me," she mumbled to herself as they continued to walk down the street. Ariana had patched up Falon a little, but they really did not have the supplies they needed to do a good job.

Ariana listened as her friend mumbled and she couldn't help but chuckle. "I thought everything went quite well. Also the Fae you were with was quite attractive, was he not?"

Falon stopped suddenly and turned to face Ariana. "He bloody stabbed me! I saved his life and he stabbed me. How's that for gratitude?" She then turned back around and started walking again. "Stupid man. Bloody visions. I couldn't have a normal best friend, oh no. Fate and its sense of humor."

Ariana chuckled again. "I should be offended, but I cannot be. When you mumble like that you sound like a little child. If it helps, I won't ask you again."

Falon looked over her shoulder, but she did not say anything else as they continued through the shadows to their destination. Finally, they made it to the house the council had told her about. Falon was getting ready to climb up the tree that was next to the house when Ariana placed her hand on her shoulder.

"Are you sure you are up to this?" Ariana asked as she watched her friend getting ready to climb up the tree onto the second story roof. It had only been an hour since Falon had gotten hurt and Ariana was afraid that she would be too weak.

Falon looked over her shoulder at Ariana and narrowed her eyes. "What do you think?" she snapped, and Ariana raised her hands in surrender. "Just keep a look out." She began to climb the tree. Ariana shook her head at her friend's stubbornness, but did what she was told.

After climbing up the tree and making her way across the second story roof to the open window, she slowly and quietly crawled in. As she came into the office she quickly looked around. She knew what she was after, but she didn't know where it was. "If I was a stack of papers where would I be?" Falon mumbled to herself. After a few more minutes of searching, she smirked as she pushed aside a bookcase to reveal a hidden nook behind it. In the nook were the papers she was looking for. "No one is creative with their hiding places anymore." She quickly put them in her bag and pushed the bookcase back.

As Falon was getting ready to climb out the window, she caught sight of something on the desk. She smiled to herself and headed back into the room, grabbing up the bag of gold with a chuckle. What kind of thief would she be if she didn't take something a little more valuable than papers?

Falon smiled as she thought about how many mouths this gold would feed. After putting the gold in her bag she quickly left the room through the window. As she made her way across the roof and down the tree, she was reminded of the pain in her side. She gritted her teeth as she hit a limb and pain shot through her. Finally, after what seemed like forever, her feet touched the ground. Once she had regained her balance, she and Ariana hurried away from the house and headed out of town.

They were about half way out of town when Fate decided to interfere with their lives yet again. Falon swore under her breath as she saw James, the bartender, being dragged toward the prison by the Witch guards.

"Great," Falon muttered as she stared after them.

"Falon, why do they have James?" Ariana asked in confusion. It wasn't like James to get into trouble. Actually, most Humans stayed out of trouble because of how harsh the Witches and Fae were to them.

"Probably because of the fight. They will want information, especially the names of us and the Fae that fought the Witches. Once they realize that he doesn't know them they will kill him because it happened in his bar." Falon put her back to the wall that she was standing beside and took a deep breath. "Go get his family and meet me in Thief's Cave. I'll meet you there as soon as I have James," Falon said, knowing that if she left James with the Witches his blood would be on her hands. She also knew that when he didn't-or rather, couldn't-give up any names, they would use his family against him. James would die, but not before watching his entire family tortured and killed.

Falon shook her head knowing that she just could not let that happen. She didn't want to have anymore blood on her hands, she had enough already.

"Good luck, my friend," Ariana said as she clasped Falon's arm. "And be careful."

"You as well." Falon went to leave, but then she stopped. Without turning around she spoke to Ariana. "If I'm not there by dawn, go home."

"I don't think so," Ariana replied before she disappeared.

Falon sighed deeply, knowing that her friend would come after her if she didn't show up to the caves by dawn. She shook her head again and hurried toward the prison. She needed to focus on retrieving James and getting out safely. It seemed to take a lifetime for Falon to arrive at the prison, but finally, she made her way into an office window. Slowly, she made her way through the halls. This was not the first time she had been in a prison, nor was it the first time she had broken into one, with each time she wished it was her last. With ever step she felt like the walls were closing in on her, trying to keep her prisoner. A shiver went down her spine as memories slowly and painfully penetrated her mind from a time when she wasn't someone breaking into prison, but a prisoner herself. Falon shook her head trying to clear it of the dread and fear that always accompanied those memories. She needed to stay focused. Staying focused was the difference between success and failure. As she hid in the shadows and waited for a guard to pass, she took control of the fear trying to take root in her mind and continued on through the dark hallways that reminded her of a never ending abyss.

Falon swore under her breath as she looked around the corner that lead to the prison cells. Her eyes fell on two guards hitting James the last of the blows sending him to the hard ground, gasping for breath. Falon leaned back and put her head against the wall. *This is going to be fun,* she thought sarcastically as she pulled out two throwing knives. She hated to kill, but she had no choice. If she left these two guards alive they would raise the alarm before she even had a chance to get James to safety. Falon quietly came around the corner and threw her knives at the two Witch guards. They stuck in their throats before they had a chance to react.

"Good throw," James rasped out as he looked up and saw the hooded figure coming towards him. He didn't know who it was and he really didn't care. If it wasn't for this stranger he would be in a lot worse condition.

Falon came over to James and helped him to his feet. When James saw her face, he was in complete shock, "Red?" This could not be the woman he had seen at his bar for the past three years. She was a Human. Humans did not go around killing Witches. Humans kept their heads down and hoped that they avoided trouble. There was just no reason to fight against a group of beings that had power when you didn't.

"Were you expecting someone else?" Falon asked giving him a small smile. "Come on, let's get out of here."

"My family. They will go after them," James said, his face and voice showing his pain.

"Goldy is getting them. They are going to meet us somewhere safe." Falon looped his arm around her neck and put her's around his waist, "They really hurt you didn't they?" James was a good man and a Human. He had no power to fight against the Witches or their abuse. Falon shook her head as she thought about the fact that so many Humans had lost their lives just because a Witch or Fae hadn't liked them. It had gotten to the point that there were very few Humans left at all.

"I'll be fine," James said, "Let's get out of here. I have spent enough time in this place to last me a life time." As they neared the door, two more Witches appeared blocking their path. "This is not good."

"This is just not my day," Falon said under her breath. She slowly moved her hand to her bag hoping that she had something left after the bar, but she knew it was a false hope. Falon rolled her eyes as she wished that Fate would give her a break just once.

"Remove your hand from that bag," one of the Witches said in a booming voice.

Falon did as he asked, as she tried to think of a way to buy more time. If she had been alone she would not worry about it, but she could not risk James getting hurt.

"Now remove that hood," the Witch ordered.

Falon closed her eyes, knowing that if this particular guard saw her face she would be in big trouble. "I think not," she said, trying to disguise her voice. *Really, Fate, can you not give me a break just this once?* Falon asked in her head as she tried to figure a way out of this situation.

As the two guards started to draw their power, Falon could see it building in their hands. "Now!" The Witch yelled at Falon as he sent a burst of power flying past Falon and James' heads. She saw James flinch out of the corner of her eye, but she didn't move. "Or do you want to be responsible for his death?" he asked pointing at James.

Falon sighed deeply, knowing that she was out of options. Slowly she moved her hand to her hood and pulled it off. Her dark red hair spilled around her shoulders, the tie that had been holding it back falling to the ground.

"Well, well. I haven't seen you in a long time, Falon," the Witch said with disgust.

"Amos." This was one Witch she could have gone her entire life without ever seeing again. *Fate, you suck,* Falon thought as she stared the Witch down. If she didn't figure a way out of this then her life was going to end very shortly, especially if Amos handed her over to Damien as he had done before.

"It has been a long time. I believe the price on your head has gone up since last we met,"

Amos said as he sauntered toward Falon and James.

Falon raised an eyebrow at him and tried not laugh. Though Amos was aiming for a menacing swagger, his walk was more of a priss. Falon couldn't help it when a laugh escaped from her. It was hard for her to take this man seriously. "So I see you still haven't mastered how to walk like a man. Is that why you always use so much power? Are you trying to over compensate for something?" Falon asked, her voice dripping with disdain. She knew she shouldn't have said it, but sometimes she just couldn't stop what came out of her mouth. She knew she had pushed him too far when he threw a bolt of power at her. "Move!" she yelled as she shoved James out of the way trying to dodge the blow. She closed her eyes, knowing that there was not enough time. She said an incantation to put up a shield, but she did know if it was enough.

~~~

Aidan looked down at the bartender and the mysterious woman from the bar. He had come to rescue the man, but it looked like the woman had beat him to it. She was really doing a number on his ego, saving him and beating him to the rescue. However, Aidan couldn't help but smirk at her courage. He had never met a Human as brave as her before. Aidan stilled as he saw the two guards approach the woman. As he watched the first blast go past her head, he felt something in him start to build. It felt like his insides were all tied up, and he wasn't sure he liked it.

Aidan looked at the woman and felt a protectiveness come over him like nothing he had ever felt before. Actually, if he were honest with himself, he would admit that he had never felt a protectiveness for anyone. He heard the guard tell her to take off her hood for the second time, and he felt his chest grow tight as the woman pulled her hood back to reveal beautiful, dark red hair. As he looked at her hair he was reminded of the glowing red embers of a fire. He shook his head, pulled his eyes away from the woman, and listened as the Witch called the woman Falon. Aidan almost laughed as Falon unmanned the Witch with her sharp wit. It had been a long time since he had enjoyed a conversation as much as he was enjoying this one. Aidan had to admit she had a quick mind and her courage knew no bounds.

Of course, the woman probably could use a bit of fear in her to keep her alive longer.

As Aidan watched he knew his time was up. He quickly jumped down and put a shield up as a blast came towards Falon. He held the shield with everything in him, knowing that he had to protect this woman even if it was just to yell at her later about her own stupidity.

~ ~ ~

Falon looked in shock at the Fae standing in front of her. What was he doing? Was he trying to protect her? "What are you doing here?" she demanded. It had been a long time since someone had tried to protect her, and she wasn't for sure if she liked it.

"Saving your life," Aidan said as he pushed the power back toward the Witch, knocking him down. He was about to do the same thing to the other when a knife flew past his shoulder and stuck in the Witch's chest. Aidan turned around and raised an eyebrow at the woman. A ghost of a smile appeared on his face as she shrugged her shoulders and turned away from him.

"I don't need saving," Falon said as she hurried over to James. She was about to help him up when the Fae grabbed her by the waist, picked her up, and set her back on her feet away from James. "What are you doing?

"That was not what it looked like from where I was, and I was moving you so I could help this man," Aidan said as he helped the man up and headed for the door.

"Maybe you should have moved so you could have gotten a better view," Falon said, her voice showing her annoyance. She hadn't needed saving in a long time. How could she have been so off today? She didn't even realize those two Witches were near until it was too late.

Aidan chuckled. "You are annoyed that I saved you." Most women would be falling at his feet thanking him. Aidan imagined that she was the type of woman who would fall at his feet to thank him, but then he shook his head. The woman in front of him would never be that type, and he was glad of it. He had, had enough of those kind of women around him to last a lifetime.

Falon stopped and looked at the Fae. "Yes. I..." She ran her hand through her hair in frustration. "Sorry. I should have said thank you. Besides, I'm not the only one who has trouble being saved," she said, her voice tinged with anger.

"I don't understand," Aidan said with confusion as they came to the door that lead to the outside. He did not know what she was talking about. When had he not handled being saved by her well? Although his ego had taken a beating, he thought he had handled it rather well.

"Did you forget that when I saved you, you stabbed me? Listen, not that I'm not enjoying this conversation, but we need to focus." Falon saw two more Witch guards a little further ahead. Normally she would avoid them, but they were near the gate that she needed to go through to get to Thief's Cave. They could go through another gate, but it would take them several hours out of their way. Falon sighed, knowing that if they did not get to the caves by dawn then Ariana would be coming after them. She had to make it to the caves. She would not risk Ariana getting caught because of two measly guards.

"We will continue this conversation later," Aidan said. He did not enjoy being reminded of the grave mistake he had made earlier. It wasn't as if she was wounded too bad, considering she was out running about rescuing people. If he had hurt her too bad she wouldn't have been able to do the things she was doing. Aidan frowned as he thought about the effect this woman was having on him. He didn't like it one bit. He also did not enjoy the way she spoke to him. Aidan was determined to have a word with her later about the patronizing tone she was using towards him. He was definitely going to have to put her in her place. No woman had ever talked to him in such a manner, and he wasn't going to let this one.

Aidan narrowed his eyes at her, but he noticed that she wasn't paying him any attention. He looked out the door to see what she was looking at and saw two Witch guards standing near the gate. "We need to go that way," Aidan said pointing to the left. He needed to get Falon and the man as far away from the guards as possible. It was only logical that they go through another gate, one that wasn't guarded.

"You do that," Falon said as she dug in her bag. She sighed knowing that if she wasn't being physically drawn to him she wouldn't be so annoyed. What was wrong with her? She had never noticed the color of a man's eyes before, but she noticed this Fae's-green with flecks of gray in them. As she looked into them, she felt drawn to him. She felt her heart skip a beat every time he stood near, and she swore he was the best-smelling man she had ever smelled before. Falon cursed in her head. Maybe the injury was causing brain damage. She shook her head to get the silly thoughts out of her mind. She did not have time for all of this nonsense. She needed to get to Thief's Cave before it was too late. The effects of losing too much blood was starting to get to her.

Aidan grabbed Falon by the arm and jerked her so she was looking at him. Anger filled him as he thought about her going toward those two guards. The only reason she had done so well in the bar was because of those devices. He knew that some Witches made devices that Humans could use with just a few words. It wasn't the Human that held the power, but the device itself. He also knew that she could throw a knife, but he was positive that it was only timing and luck that had given her victory on both accounts. Aidan knew that if he hadn't intervened in the prison, she would now be captured or dead. With her sassy mouth he would lean more towards dead.

"I don't have time for your insolence. We are going the way I said. I won't have you die because you don't know how to use your head."

Falon felt her eyes turn red as his grip on her tightened. She tried to let the anger go so that her eyes would not change, but she could not. She didn't know if it was because he dared to touch her, or that the idea of him being angry at her was upsetting to her. She had never cared if someone was angry at her, and she wasn't going to start now... no matter how beautiful his eyes were or how much she longed to feel his arms around her. *Oh, where the hell did that come from?!* Falon thought her anger rising to another level. She forgot all about control as she spoke to Aidan. "Get your hand off me."

Aidan had never seen eyes like Falon's before. They intrigued him. All the Humans he had known in the past had one set eye color. Even Witches' and Fae's eyes did not change. "Your eyes are turning red."

"That means I'm angry. Now. Let. Me. Go," Falon said, speaking to him through clenched teeth.

Aidan let go of Falon's arm and stared at her. He tilted his head, trying to figure out exactly what had happened. As he watched her take deep breaths, he saw her eyes turn back to their normal deep brown. Although Aidan like the warm brown color of her eyes, he had really like the red, though he didn't understand why.

Aidan cleared his throat and cleared his mind. "You need to come with me. I'll get you safely out of the city."

"No, my friend is going to meet us with James' family in Thief's Cave." Falon pointed to the gates. "I need to go that way to get to the caves. If we go out any other gates it will take too long. I only have until dawn before my friend comes after me."

"Listen, my friend went to help James' family as well. He will take her to the most logical choice. He will also make sure she does not leave until I get there." If he let her go at all Aidan thought. He pictured Cale's face when he had noticed that the women had disappeared.

When Cale got the woman back he was not going to be letting her out of his sight. "Besides, there are two guards that way. How do you suggest we get rid of them? Do you have any more tricks in that bag? If I use my magic we will have more guards on top of us before we can even finish off those two. Plus, I'm the only one here *with* magic, and I'm not risking over-taxing myself because you want to have a shorter walk."

Falon raised an eyebrow at him, taking off her cloak and bag. Aidan felt his mouth fall open as he took in her tight black leather pants, and black corset that she wore over white shirt. He eyed the laces that held her shirt closed at her chest. He had never seen a woman dressed the way she was. If a woman did not wear a dress then she wore men's clothing, but not in this manner. Aidan licked his lips as he noticed her figure. She really was a beautiful woman. As he looked her up and down, he wondered how many other men had seen her dressed in such attire. For some reason the thought made his blood boil.

Aidan's anger-and for lack of a better word, desire turned into pure shock as he watched her begin to untie the laces to the top of her shirt.

46

"What...what are you doing?" He felt his mouth go dry as the laces gave way and most of her chest was exposed for him to see. What the hell was she thinking showing that much of herself?! "You...You..." Aidan stumbled over his words not knowing what to say. It was as if his tongue had forgotten how to work. That, or his brain. He quickly grabbed her cloak and tried to wrap it around her shoulders to cover her up. He realized that he was not the only one seeing her chest. He gave a quick glare at James, who actually didn't look too interested before turning back to Falon, who was looking at him with an annoyed look on her face.

"I took my cloak off for a reason. Now will you hold on to this for me?" she asked, handing him her bag then taking off the cloak again.

Aidan growled as he saw her exposed flesh again. It wasn't as if he wasn't enjoying the view, but he did not like the idea of *other men* enjoying the view. He shook his head. He had never been a possessive man, and he wasn't going to start with some Human woman. He needed to figure out what was wrong with himself and get over it. He had things to do, and they did not involve getting tangled up with this stubborn, annoying woman. "Put that back on. You are not decent," he snapped as he once again tried to cover her up.

"Just hold it, will you? Listen, I'll put it back on in a moment. Just wait here. I'll be right back." Falon gave him a sassy smile then walked off.

"Get back here!" he hissed. He felt his gut tighten as he watched her walk towards the two Witches. What was she doing? She was going to get herself killed. Aidan didn't know what to do. If he called out to her any louder he would be heard and if he went after her they would be caught.

Falon walked towards the Witches, her hips swaying as she did. She needed to make herself look drunk and easy. With her tight leather pants and unlaced top she was definitely pulling it off. All she had to do now was be convincing. Of course, that was going to be difficult because the idea of getting anywhere close enough to pull off what she had to was already making her sick to her stomach. "You can do this," she said under her breath as she continued towards the Witches. It would only take a moment and then she would re-lace her shirt and put her cloak back on. She tried to look as confident as possible. Well, as confident as a drunk woman could look.

"Lookie what we have here," one of the men said as Falon stumbled into him. She smiled up at him sweetly.

"I seem to be lost," she said slurring her words together. "Can you take me home?" She looked at him coyly batting her eyelashes. She had seen some women do these things at home, but she had never tried them herself. To be honest, she really did not understand the whole process of getting a man. She had not bothered with it, considering no man would ever want to be with her full time anyway. Of course, there were always those looking for a one night stand, but she wasn't interested in that.

"I can do better than that. I'll take you home with me," the other Witch said as he pulled her by the waist into his arms.

Falon felt like she was going to be sick as he leaned down, kissed her neck, and cupped her butt with his hands. "I think you should sleep," Falon said fighting panic as she felt his hand inch up her body. She said a quick incantation and watched as both Witches fell asleep at her feet. She hoped that hurt like hell.

Aidan felt an anger and jealousy rise in him like he had never felt before as he watched that Witch put his hands on Falon's butt. He was thinking about heading over there and ripping the man's hands off when James grabbed his arm.

"She said to stay here." He could tell by the look on his face that he was not happy with what Falon was doing. He wasn't happy about it much either, but he also knew that the girl could take care of herself. He had seen plenty of proof of that.

Aidan glared at James and was about to use his power to push him away when he saw the Witches drop to the ground, unconscious. He turned his head to see Falon re-lacing her shirt and walking towards him. "What were you thinking?!"

"I was thinking that the guards needed to be taken care of, so I took care of them. Listen, I'm on a time frame." Falon grabbed her cloak that had fallen to the ground and put it back on. She then grabbed her bag from the Fae. "Are we just going to stand here or are we going to go?"

"Do you know what they could have done to you?" He took her by the shoulders giving her a small shake. Why was it that this Human took so many risks? Did she not think about her own safety?

Falon shrugged his hands off and looked up into his eyes. "I can take care of myself. I have been doing it for some time now." She turned and headed the direction of the gates. It was still going to be a couple of hours before they arrived at Thief's Cave, and she wasn't for sure if she had the energy to make it. She closed her eyes as she tried to block out the pain.

Aidan watched her leave in annoyance. He wondered if she was worth looking after, but in the end he just sighed and started walking.

"Cale, I'm going to kill you when I see you again." His mood lightened as he thought about all the different ways he could kill Cale once they were back together.

Chapter Three

"I don't think you know where you are going," Aidan said stiffly as he looked around to make sure they weren't being followed.

Falon rolled her eyes. This was the tenth time Aidan had criticized her sense of direction in just a few minutes. "I know where I'm going. I'm just making sure we aren't being followed. Now, will you please stop saying that." Falon approached a tree, placed her hand on the trunk, and leaned against it. She was tired, in pain, and this Fae was getting on her nerves. She closed her eyes to get her breathing under control.

"No one is following us," Aidan said not noticing how pale Falon was or how tired she looked. All Aidan was thinking about was how he wished she would take her hood off again so he could see her dark red hair. Aidan shook his head, anger filling him. He needed to get a grip. There was no reason for him to be this attracted to her. She was a Human. Aidan was so lost in his thoughts that it took him a minute to notice that Falon was leaning weakly against a tree with James standing next to her. "Are you all right? What happened?" he asked as he approached her.

"Yes, it's nothing. Just need to catch my breath," Falon said, trying not to let the pain show in her voice. She was going to have to lay down soon if she wanted to regain her strength.

Aidan came to stand in front of her. It was then that he noticed the paleness of her skin and the sweat that had formed on her brow. He slowly brushed a stray piece of hair out of her face. "You're pale. Very pale." He looked her up and down trying to find any sort of injury. The only reason for her to be this pale was that she had an injury and had lost a lot of blood. Guilt filled him as he thought about when she had saved him. He closed his eyes as he pictured it in his head. If he wasn't mistaken he had cut her on her left lower side. Aidan opened his eyes and started to push back her cloak. He needed to look at her wound so he could see how much damage he had done.

Damn, he felt like a complete idiot for hurting her. She had saved his life and he had repaid her by stabbing her.

"What are you doing?" Falon asked as she pushed his hand away. She was not in the mood for this Fae to try to touch her. She had enough feelings flowing through her without him manhandling her. She couldn't imagine what it would be like if he did touch her.

"Let me see," Aidan said as he looked into her eyes. Looking into their depths made him feel like he could do anything. It made him feel like happy endings could exist. Looking into them made him want to believe in a future that couldn't exist. That would never exist.

Falon looked away breaking the spell that he seemed to hold over her, the spell that made her want to believe in something that wasn't real. She had dreamed long ago of a man who would make her world a better place, but it had all been a lie. A beautiful lie. There was no such man and there were no happily-ever-afters. Falon shook her head and tried to forget the feelings he was causing within her. It was as if he was bringing her hardened heart back to life. He was making her believe in the lies they tell you as a child. The things you want to believe will come true, but deep in your heart you know they won't.

"I'm fine. Besides, I don't let men that I don't know examine me," Falon said with a slight smirk. "Especially, if I don't even know their names." She was growing weaker. She needed to get her side dealt with properly, and she needed to get away from this Fae. Maybe it was the loss of blood that was causing her to be so confused. So drawn to him. Yes it was just the loss of blood. It wasn't anything else. Falon looked at Aidan again and when their eyes met, she knew she was in big trouble. If this was Fate's idea of a joke bringing her together with a Fae then Fate had another thing coming. She would never give into these feelings, and she would never give into this Fae. "Listen, the caves are just a little further. I'll be fine until then." With what little strength she had left, she pushed herself away from the tree and continued on. As she walked she looked over her shoulder at James and Aidan. "You two coming? Or are you just going to look at me like I'm crazy?"

"Coming," James said as he hurried after her. "I'm ready to see my family."

"I'm sure you are. I promise they are safe. Goldy would have gotten them to safety." Falon patted James on the shoulder then hurried ahead.

Aidan came to walk beside her. He was impressed by her strength and determination. She was unlike any woman he had ever met before. "Aidan."

"What?" Falon asked, confused.

"My name is Aidan," he said as he helped her over a fallen log. Aidan was stunned when she didn't pull back from him. "You really are not feeling well, are you?" It was his fault she was in pain. She had saved him, and he had repaid her by attacking. True, it had only been a reflex, but that did not excuse it.

"I'll be fine." Falon walked a little more then stumbled. Aidan grabbed her arm and steadied her. She knew he was about to say something so she spoke first. "Your name. I like it."

Aidan looked at her with his eyebrows scrunched, but he didn't say anything about her stumbling. "Thanks. I like Falon."

Falon nodded then looked over her shoulder at James. "You all right back there?"

"I'm fine. Just worrying. How much longer?" James asked as he caught up to them.

"Just a few more minutes. So, do you like it?"

"Like what?" James asked trying to understand what she was talking about. For most of the trip he had been lost in his own thoughts about his family and not paying attention to their conversation. Of course, most of the time all three of them had been quiet. The few times they had spoken, it was usually the Fae asking if Falon was lost.

"His name. It's Aidan. I like it. Come, we are almost there. It is just on the other side of those bushes."

She felt herself get dizzy as she bent down and entered the entrance to the cave that was hidden behind the bushes. Her dizziness caused her to be unprepared as a hand shot out of the darkness, grabbed her by the throat, and slammed her against the cave wall. Falon felt pain shoot through her side then her weakness set in, causing everything to go black.

"Get your hands off her!" Aidan yelled as he grabbed the dark figure from behind and threw him away from Falon. He turned and saw Falon hit the ground and lie still. Anger filled him as he turned back to the figure. No one had the right to touch what was his. The thought came from nowhere, and Aidan tamped down on it immediately.

"Aidan?" Cale asked as he pushed himself up off the ground.

"Falon!" Ariana yelled out as she hurried over to her friend, who was laying motionless on the cave floor. "Falon, look at me." She rolled Falon over so that she could see her face. As she looked at Falon, she realized how pale she was. Ariana heard Cale's friend come up behind her, but she didn't take her eyes off Falon, "Come on. Look at me."

"Move." Aidan grabbed Falon's friend by the waist and moved her out of the way. He then knelt next to Falon. "Wake up," he said as he patted her face with his hand. When she didn't stir, worry filled him. He quickly pushed her cloak aside and looked down to her side. He should have forced her to let him see her wound earlier. What if he was too late? No, he thought, shaking his head. She was going to be fine as soon as he took care of her. "Cale, do you have your pack with you?" He looked down at her side and felt his blood run cold. A lot of Falon's blood had seeped through the makeshift bandage. "Cale?!"

He grabbed his pack and hurried over to Aidan. "Here," he said as he knelt next to them. "I did not mean her harm. I was just protecting those with me."

Aidan grabbed the bag and spoke with out looking at Cale. "I know. It isn't you that hurt her. You just added to the problem," he said as he pulled out some medical supplies. He quickly cut away Falon's corset so he could get to her wound before pushing up her shirt and tending to it. It only took him a few minutes, but he knew it would take much longer for her to regain her strength. She had lost a lot of blood, but not as much as he had first thought. The bandage and the corset had kept her from losing too much. "We need to get her somewhere dry and safe. She needs rest," Aidan said as he pulled her shirt back down and wrapped her more securely in her cloak. He didn't want her to get a chill on top of everything else.

"Will she be all right?" Ariana asked as she knelt down next to her friend. She brushed a lock of hair out of her face. "She's so pale." She shook her head as Falon's words from earlier entered her mind. Falon had said that she always seemed to get hurt when Ariana had visions. Ariana thought about it for a moment, and she realized that Falon was right. Ariana sighed sadly and looked down at her friend. Why couldn't she be a seer like the ones from the past? Why were her visions always so confusing?

"She will be fine with rest," Aidan said as he looked at the blond woman next to him. "Who are you?"

"Ariana," she answered with a small smile. She knew that her vision may have gotten Falon hurt, but she also knew without a doubt that the Fae looking at her was Falon's mate. He was the only one who could ever truly get to Falon's heart.

"I'm Aidan. You are a Witch?"

"Yes." She stood, watching as Aidan lifted Falon gently into his arms.

"How did a Witch and Human become friends?" Aidan asked as he looked around the cave. He noticed that James had been reunited with his family.

"It's a long story," Ariana said with a small smile.

"Very well. Listen, she needs somewhere safe to rest." He looked down at Falon. For some reason, he really enjoyed having her in his arms. It just felt right and familiar. It felt like a dream he had held onto for so long.

"This way," Ariana said as she headed deeper into the cave.

"It will be too cold for her in there. We must go somewhere else," Aidan said as his grip tightened on Falon. He kept telling himself that the only reason he was worried about her was because he was the one who had hurt her. It was a very logical response. *Yeah keep telling yourself that,* Aidan thought with a grimace.

"Trust me. I would not do anything to make her worse. She's my best friend," Ariana said sweetly. "We must go further in the cave."

Aidan nodded, then followed Cale and his mate. Ariana. He needed to remember that name. It would be rude to just call her Cale's mate. Aidan saw Cale look over at Ariana as she gave his friend the most loving and charming smile he had ever seen. His heart suddenly tightened as he thought about Falon looking at him like that. For some reason, he longed for that, or for just a smile from her that would break the walls around his heart. "Damn fool," Aidan said under his breath. He cleared his mind from such silly daydreams. He was a Fae bounty hunter who had given up on finding a mate years ago. He was not about to start having stupid feelings for a Human woman who couldn't stay out of trouble.

"Pardon?" Ariana asked as she heard Aidan mumbling. This Fae was very different from Cale. Cale was more open and light while Aidan seemed to hide a dark side. Maybe he wasn't the best one to have around her friend. Falon needed some light in her life, not more darkness.

"He mumbles to himself. You'll get used to it," Cale said as he came up and put his arm around Ariana's shoulders.

"Falon does that as well. Usually when she is aggravated." Ariana's smile faded, "She'll be fine, won't she?"

"Yes," Aidan said as they went deeper into the caves. After a while they came to a dead end. "I thought you said you knew where you were going!" he yelled.

Falon woke up to realize two things: one, she was in Aidan's arms and two, he was extremely angry. Funnily enough it was the first fact that bothered her the most. Just the feel of his arms holding her body against his was sending pulses of electricity throughout her whole body. "Can you put me down?" Falon asked, her voice not much more than a whisper.

Aidan looked down, frowning when he saw how pale Falon was. "No, you need to rest."

Falon tilted her head at him in confusion. She was about to say something when Aidan's friend spoke up.

Cale stepped in front of Ariana, "You won't raise your voice at her," he said his jaw clenched. Cale knew that Aidan was angry, but he didn't understand why. They had been in similar situations before and Aidan had never acted like this, especially not toward a female. So why was he acting so weird now?

"Why are you yelling at my friend?" Falon asked with a frown, looking up at Aidan. No one had a right to yell at her friend but her. Falon almost chuckled at the logic of that thought, but she contained herself.

"Because she is incompetent," Aidan said not looking away from Cale and Ariana. How could she had led them further into the cave with nowhere else for them to go? Was she really that stupid of a Witch?

"You shouldn't have said that," Ariana said softly as she looked at Aidan with a grimace. This was not good.

"Why no-" Before Aidan could finish his question he was flying backwards across the cave and hit the wall. *What the hell had just happened?* Aidan thought as he shook his head and looked up from where he had landed after hitting the wall.

Falon hit the floor as Aidan flew backwards. She hissed and grabbed her side. "That was a bad idea," she winced as the pain engulfed her. It took everything in her not to give into the darkness that wanted to claim her.

"Falon, you need to think before you act," Ariana said as she came to her friend's side.

"Yeah, yeah," Falon muttered through clenched teeth. "Help me up." She was finally able to regain her breath and push the darkness aside and with Ariana's help, she stood on shaky legs. Falon looked to where Cale was helping Aidan off the floor. She smirked as she saw the bewildered look on Aidan's face. Maybe now he would be more hesitant about yelling at Ariana and calling her names. She would never let anyone talk to Ariana like Aidan had.

"What was that?" Aidan asked as Cale helped him up. He shook his head trying to clear it. He hadn't felt that much power in a long time.

"That was you angering the wrong woman," Cale said trying not to laugh. His friend looked truly confused.

"Falon?" Aidan asked as they walked over to the girls. Why would Falon have thrown him across the room when she had been in his arms? Was she that stupid? "Falon!"

"What?" she snapped. She squared her shoulders and gave Aidan a look that dared him to continue this conversation, as Aidan spoke, Falon knew that she apparently needed to work on that look some more.

"What were you thinking?!" he yelled as he got in Falon's face. He was surprised when she didn't flinch or back down. It had been a long time since someone had stood up to him like this. He had a habit of even making Cale back down from time to time and Cale was his friend. Why was this Human woman not scared of him? What made her so special? Did she not fear anything? Maybe it was that she was too dumb to fear him. Yeah that made him feel better. Maybe this stupid attraction would soon disappear.

"I was thinking I don't like people insulting my friend. Now if you would have given her an opportunity she would have shown you the way out." Falon moved away from them all slowly and placed her hand on the wall. With a few words the wall opened up to reveal a hidden room.

Falon turned and glared at Aidan not saying anything, but her eyes told him how angry she was and how stupid she thought he was at the moment. Great, now she thought he was an idiot. Aidan rubbed the back of his neck in frustration.

Cale watched as James, his family, Falon, and Ariana went into the room, "I think you have met you match," Cale said with a laugh.

"Stubborn woman," Aidan said to himself as he followed the group in. He was amazed when he stepped into a large room. Aidan looked around and saw that off to the side were open doors leading to more rooms. Why was there a place like this in a cave? "Why is this here?" he asked as he watched James light a fire. "What is this place?"

"It's a place to rest and hide. A place for thieves," Falon said as she slowly sat down in a chair. She felt the tiredness and pain all the way to her bones. She leaned her head back. She could use a good nap, but she knew she needed to get defenses up. After that she would be able to rest. Falon was about to stand up when Aidan came over to her. Falon let out an annoyed sigh. She was really not in the mood for him right now. A part of her wanted his comfort, but the other part wanted to snap his head off, and she knew the snappy part would win out.

Aidan's anger left and concern replaced it as he saw Falon wince, "Let me see if you did anymore damage to yourself," he ordered.

"I have had enough of your help. Thank you very much." Her voice showed her anger. She refused to open her eyes and give Aidan the satisfaction of seeing the pain. Why couldn't he just leave her alone? Why had Fate brought him into her life? Stupid Fate.

"I'm not the one who hurt herself because she didn't use the brain in her head. Now let me look!" he demanded getting aggravated. What was her problem? He was just trying to help her. Aidan stopped for a moment and thought about how he would be reacting if someone had insulted his best friend. Aidan's eyebrows scrunched together as he realized that Falon was actually not behaving too awful considering the circumstances.

Falon stood up, ignoring the pain and the dizziness that was causing her to lose her balance. "Push through this," she thought as she got in Aidan's face. "I don't have many friends and I don't allow anyone to insult them. I protect what is mine," Falon said.

Aidan could not help it when his lips curved at the edges in a ghost of a smile. He admired her spunk and fire. He also loved it when her brown eyes seemed to take on a red tint. "You don't fear me. Do you?" Aidan's smile faded and shock took it's place as he realized that this mere Human woman didn't fear him, when some of the most powerful beings of this world did.

Falon scoffed, "No. Should I?" she asked with a sarcastic tone.

"Possibly," he said as he got even closer. It would do her some good to fear him. He watched as her lips quirked up in a quick smile, but it was soon gone, as her face grew ghost white and her eyes closed.

Falon couldn't help the small smile that spread across her face, but she knew it faded quickly. As she stood there she thought about commenting, but the the room began to sway and the darkness again tried to claim her.

Aidan watched as Falon swayed and her knees gave out. He quickly scooped her up in his arms. "Cale!" Aidan yelled as he hurried her into another room.

"Do you always shout?" Falon asked with a smile before everything went black.

Aidan looked down as Falon went limp in his arms. His heart tightened as he saw the color leave her face. She looked like a ghost, she was so white. "Cale!" Aidan hurried over to one of the beds and gently laid her down. He brushed a piece of hair out of her face. He felt her forehead and knew that she was suffering from a fever. She was going to need some medicine to stop the spread of any kind of infection. Aidan cursed himself as he realized he hadn't even thought of that earlier. She was probably going to need a new bandage considering she was bleeding again. Aidan lifted her shirt and looked at the bandage. He was about to remove it when Cale came into the room with his bag.

"I'm here. Let me look at her," Cale said as he tried to get to Falon.

"No, I'll do it," Aidan said not wanting anyone else to look at Falon. He couldn't explain his jealousy and right now he didn't care. All he cared about was making sure Falon was all right.

"Aidan, I have more experience with healing. Let me help her," Cale said softly. Aidan had met his mate. Cale wondered what Aidan would do once he came to the realization that Falon was his mate. He would probably have a heart attack considering his mate was a Human and one that seemed to get into a lot of trouble.

Aidan finally relented and moved away from Falon. In his mind he knew that Cale was a much better healer, but he still had trouble moving away from her. As Aidan looked around the room, he saw Ariana's worried face peeking in through the door. He couldn't help but smile when Ariana spoke.

"She always has been stubborn. She doesn't think before she acts. She also hates getting help, as much as, she hates showing any kind of weakness." Ariana wrapped her arms around her waist as she watched Cale work on Falon. "I'll fix every one something to eat."

"Cale is a good healer. She'll be fine." Aidan cleared his throat, "And I apologize for earlier. I should..."

Ariana held up her hand to stop him. "Don't worry over it. Just look after Falon for me." Ariana walked out of the room. Instead of focusing and worrying about Falon, he listened as Ariana and James' wife spoke to one another. He was shocked when she let her and Falon take the blame for what happened in the bar, but not as shocked as he was when she offered James and his family a new home. Aidan had been wondering what he was going to do with them, but had not come up with any ideas. Aidan continued to listen hoping for anything of value to hold onto. He didn't know where Falon's home was or what it was. If a Witch was living with Humans peacefully than it was definitely an odd place. In most places Humans were seen as dirt, scum, but Ariana treated them as her equals. She had definitely been raised differently or maybe it was having a Human for a best friend. Maybe it had been Falon who had changed her way of thinking. She was definitely screwing up his way of thinking. Aidan lost himself in his thoughts as he stared at Falon. He stopped listening to Ariana. Why did this Human have such a pull on him? Aidan stared at Falon until Cale came over to him.

"She will be fine with some rest. She is one tough Human," Cale said as he looked at his friend. "I'm going to go get something to eat. Would you like me to bring you something?"

Aidan nodded yes and went over to Falon's side. He sat down in the chair that Cale had brought over. He didn't know how long he sat there just staring at her when Ariana entered the room and brought him back to reality.

Ariana entered the room and she smiled as she saw Aidan sitting next to her friend. "I brought you something to eat."

Aidan looked at Ariana and took the bowl out of her hand, "Thank you."

"You do have manners," A soft voice said from the bed.

Ariana looked over at Falon. "He is not the only one who has forgotten about manners," she said with a small smile, "I'll go get you something to eat."

"Not right now, but thank you," Falon said weakly.

Ariana looked over at her and nodded. Falon watched as her friend disappeared into the other room, "she is right, I have been rude." Falon closed her eyes and sighed.

"I noticed you didn't apologize," Aidan said with a smirk. He had not expected one, but it was fun to tease her. Again Aidan wondered what was wrong with himself. He had never been the teasing or playful sort, but something about her changed that. He wanted to bring a smile to her face, a smile that would light up those dark brown eyes.

Falon opened her eyes and looked at Aidan with a small smile. "I don't apologize, but I'll try to do better." Falon went to push herself up, but Aidan stopped her.

"You should rest," Aidan said. Most people, let alone, a woman would not stand up to him. "You lost a lot of blood."

Falon chuckled, "I have been hurt worse than this." She slowly sat up. She closed her eyes pushing the pain out of her mind. When she opened her eyes she could see the worry on Aidan's face. "It has been a long time since some one has worried about me," Falon said not knowing if she liked him worrying about her or not.

Aidan frowned as her words penetrated his brain. Worried. Was he worried about her? No, he wasn't worried. Because if he was worried, it would mean that he cared for her, even if it was just a little. "I'm not worried. If you want to injure yourself further than that is your business," he said his voice harsh and cold. He wasn't worried about her, some Human. Why would he be? Aidan hardly ever worried about Cale so he wasn't going to worry about this stupid woman who didn't know how to take care of herself. Some woman that in a few days he would never see again. Aidan's gut tightened at that thought. He didn't like the idea of never seeing her again.

Falon looked at Aidan and wondered what was going through his head. "I'm glad you aren't worried." Falon slowly stood up, but with the loss of blood she swayed a little. "Push it aside," she thought. She would rest once she knew everyone was safe for the night.

"You are being an idiot. You must be out of your mind if you are already trying to get up," Aidan said harshly as he grabbed her arm and steadied her.

"Possibly, but there's much that needs to be done. I'll rest once I know everyone is safe for the night." Falon closed her eyes and took a deep breath. Once she knew she was steady she pulled her arm away from Aidan, "Thank you for your assistance." She left the room leaving Aidan staring after her.

"I don't care if she bleeds to death. I don't care. Stupid woman," Aidan said to himself, but even as the words left his mouth he knew they were a lie. He was worried about this woman and he didn't know why. In his mind images of her kept invading his thoughts, so he put his bowl down and hurried after her. "Let me at least help you," he said as he came over to her leaning against the wall.

"Thank you, but no. I have to push through it. I'm stronger than this," Falon said closing her eyes. She imagined herself healing if only just a little. She normally could not heal herself like she could heal others, but she was able to give herself more strength. After a few minutes she felt strength go through her body. It would only last a few hours, but that would be enough time to set up the defenses, then she would rest. Of course, it would leave her more tired than if she just regained her strength naturally.

"You have grown very pale," Aidan said as he brushed a piece of hair out of her face. "You should lay back down." Maybe a new approach on it would help. Maybe if he suggested, instead of demanding it would help.

"I will, once I have the defenses up." Falon opened her eyes and gave him a small smile. "Go eat. I'll be back shortly."

"Of course, it didn't work," Aidan said as he threw up his hands and watched as Falon walked through yet another secret door. Before he could follow Ariana came up behind him.

"She is stubborn but she knows her own strength. She also takes her job of protection very seriously."

"How will she put up defenses? She is a Human, not a Witch or Fae," Aidan asked as he turned towards Cale's mate. She really was pretty, but not as pretty as Falon. Plus she did not have as much fire. Aidan shook his head in aggravation. This was ridiculous. He should not be thinking of Falon like this. Nothing could ever happen between them. Fae could only ever be with their mates, and his mate was long gone.

Ariana tilted her head and looked at Aidan. "She has a Witch's stone that she wears around her neck."

"A Witch's stone?!" Aidan asked in a shout, "Where did she get one of those? All of those were suppose to have been destroyed a thousand years ago."

"Where she got it is her business," Ariana said with a raised eyebrow. "and there is no reason to yell. If you have something you wish to take up with Falon then do it with her not me. I was just answering your question." Ariana then walked off holding back her smile until her back was to Aidan. She wondered how much longer Aidan was going to fight the inevitable.

Aidan clenched his jaw and fists then walked out of the secret door. He was going to have a lot to say to Falon once he saw her. Aidan swore under his breath as he thought about Falon using a Witch's stone. They were stones that contained the power of dying Witches. Any wearer could call on that power and use it but they were made for Witches not Humans. Aidan hurried through the tunnel that had been behind the door. He just knew that he was going to find Falon passed out or dead. Witch's Stones took a lot of strength and they weren't meant for Humans. "I can't believe Falon has one of those? And that she is using it to put up the defenses!" Aidan yelled out to himself as he finally came to the end of the tunnel.

Aidan stepped out into the open air and looked around for Falon. Finally, his eyes fell on her sitting on the ground, her back to a tree, her breathing labored. "Are you all right?" Aidan asked as he came closer to her.

"Fine," Falon said not opening her eyes.

Aidan knelt in front of her and pulled out her necklace. It was an orange stone on a sliver necklace. "This could kill you!" He yelled.

Falon took a deep breath trying not to lose her temper, "there is no need to shout, I'm not deaf."

"No, but you are lacking in intelligence. Those stones should not be used by a Human. Especially, one who is in your condition. These things were made for Witches," he said with a growl as he grabbed her by the shoulders and shook her.

Falon opened her eyes and tilted her head to look at Aidan. "I don't understand you. You get angry over the silliest things. I have had this necklace for as long as I can remember, and I handle the power just fine. Maybe you should not underestimate me or lump me into the typical Human group." Falon shook her head and chuckled. She went to stand up, but Aidan stopped her.

"You'll be weak after using that stone," Aidan said slowly as if she was a child. Why could she not see how weak she was?

"I'm not a child so don't speak to me as if I'm one," Falon said the anger in her growing. "And just because I'm a woman and a...Human does not mean that I'm weak." Falon shoved Aidan backwards, but before he fell to far he grabbed her wrist and pulled her down on top of him. He quickly rolled her on her back and secured her hands above her head.

"It is a known fact that woman are weaker than men," Aidan said as he stared down at her. Every sense he had was alert to the fact that he was pressed against Falon so intimately. Man, she was beautiful. Did he really think that he had seen a woman more beautiful than her? What had he been thinking?

Falon narrowed her eyes and before Aidan knew what was happening she brought her leg up and wrapped it around his. She used it to push him over onto his back. Once she had him on his back she put a knife to his throat. "I have been taking care of myself since I was five. I don't need a man or anyone else to look after me."

Aidan felt the blade at his throat and was impressed. "Not many people get the better of me."

Falon scoffed, shoved off of him, and stood up. "Listen I'm sure you and Cale have somewhere else to be. Why don't you leave?" Falon asked knowing that Ariana would never let Cale go, but she could hope. "Come on Fate for once be on my side," Falon thought to herself.

Aidan stood up, dusted his leather pants off, and Falon couldn't help but admire him. He really was quite attractive. Falon shook her head and began to walk away. She didn't have the time or the inclination to get involved with any one. Her life was way too complicated to involve anyone else in it. Before Falon got too far Aidan had grabbed her, turned her around, and pinned her to a tree. "Never turn your back on an enemy unless you know they won't get back up again," he said his face just mere inches from Falon's. His eyes locked with hers then slowly they moved down until they were staring intently at her mouth. Suddenly, the urge to kiss her was overwhelming him.

Falon swallowed trying not to let the closeness of his body affect her, "Are you an enemy?" she asked her voice coming out sounding a little breathless. She wanted him to say yes, but she also wanted him to say no.

What was wrong with her? She didn't even know her own mind anymore.

"No," Aidan said quietly then his eyes locked once again with hers. Falon felt her heart race as Aidan leaned closer to her. She knew he was going to kiss her, and she couldn't let it happen. Before she could make up her mind or become even more confused she pushed at him with her powers knocking him to the ground. She laughed as she saw the look on his face. "Sorry," Falon said with a mock innocence, "I don't know how that could have possibly happened. Especially, since I'm so weak." She then smiled sweetly at him and walked back into the cave.

Aidan waited until she was gone then burst out laughing. Cale was right, he had finally met his match. "Well let the game begin," Aidan thought as he wondered what their next confrontation was going to be like. Aidan smiled, looking forward to the challenge.

Chapter Four

Falon had come inside the cave hoping to get some rest but after several hours she still couldn't sleep. Falon put her finger tips to her temples as a headache started to form behind her eyes. "Falon, why don't you sing your song. Maybe it will sooth the children," Ariana begged her voice not as sweet sounding as normal. Of course, after four hours of listening to the child cry she was not feeling very nice towards the child either, and she normally loved children, but this was pushing it. "Please, Falon, I can't take much more of this."

"I'll try." Falon stood up and walked over to Teresa.

"I'm so sorry, I don't know what's wrong with her," Teresa said as she tried to get her daughter to stop crying.

"May I?" Falon asked holding out her hands for the baby, "I have found that when you are stressed your baby can sense it." Teresa handed little Chloe over to Falon.

Aidan was curious to see how Falon was planning on taking care of the child. He had thought of interfering for the past few minutes, but he didn't think the Human would approve. As he watched Falon with the child something in him changed. Something in him melted as he watched her rock the child in her arms. Aidan leaned back against the wall and waited for the song that Ariana had asked Falon to sing.

As Falon took the baby into her arms she could sense that the baby was ill. Without letting anyone know what she was doing she pushed her energy through the child healing her. She began to sing a song that she had known her whole life. As she sang the child drifted off to sleep healed and whole.

Aidan moved away from the wall as soon as Falon started to sing. He felt like he was in a dream as Falon began to sing the song that had been in his dreams for years. The song that had haunted him for so long. This was impossible. His mate was not supposed to exist anymore.

She was supposed to have died years ago. Aidan shook his head and finally opened his mind to Falon. He looked into Falon's eyes, and he knew she was his mate. Suddenly, it felt like his air was being cut off as he looked at his mate. A Human. This stubborn, sarcastic woman was his mate. Aidan left the room trying not to panic. Falon was his mate. A woman who was a magnet for trouble. Aidan hurried through the tunnel, and he leaned against a tree trying to catch his breath. "This can't be happening," he said to no one in particular. Aidan ran his hands down his face. "Fate you have a wicked sense of humor." Hell he was angry. He was really angry. Not only was his mate a Human, but she was stubborn and didn't know when she needed help or how to be careful.

"How does it feel?" Cale asked as he came over next to his friend and leader.

"How does what feel?" Aidan asked as he looked up at the stars trying to clear his mind and get some control over his emotions. How had his life gotten so messed up? Oh yeah it was his dumb idea of going into a Witch town, into a Witch bar to get a stupid Witch. Who he ended up not getting anyway.

"Finding your mate," Cale said with a small smile.

Aidan was about to deny it, but in the end he decided against it, "She is a Human who does not know how to stay out of trouble or know how to use the head that is on her shoulders. How did I end up with one so stubborn and annoying as my mate? Is this punishment for the things I've done in my life?" Aidan asked as he turned and looked at Cale, "You get the sweet, good tempered one, and I get the fiery, stubborn, angry one."

Cale laughed, "I have been better behaved than you but think about it. If you were with a woman like Ariana you would run all over her. With Falon you don't have to worry about that."

Aidan laughed, "yes, I just have to worry about her running over me and getting herself killed. This should be interesting. She's going to be the death of me. I can just feel it. Besides this isn't the way it was suppose to be. The prophecy said that I was to end up with a Fire Elemental. When we had to fight them I gave up the hope of ever finding my mate. I just don't understand."

Cale laughed, "maybe the prophecy was false and as for the other part you always did love a challenge. Besides do you know how long it has been since I've heard you laugh?"

Aidan looked at him in shock, "I laugh."

Cale shook his head then walked back into the cave. Aidan stared back at the stars lost in thought. He and Cale were going to have to stay with their mates. This was going to change their lives completely.

"You look lost in your thoughts."

Aidan turned around to see Falon come up behind him. She looked tired. "I was. You should be resting not out walking around," Aidan said without smiling. Just because she was his mate didn't mean he had to like it or change himself. No, she was going to have be the one doing the changing before they ever had a relationship.

"I'm going to rest later, but right now I need some quiet time. I'll leave you to your thoughts." Falon headed deeper into the forest. Aidan sighed knowing that he couldn't let her go off on her own. That woman seemed to find trouble everywhere. Aidan kicked a rock with his foot, sighed deeply, then followed after her. If she was his mate he might as well keep her safe.

Falon could hear that Aidan was following her, but she didn't care. "I thought you were going back to your thoughts?" Falon asked without looking behind you.

"I thought I should follow you instead. You do have a habit of getting in trouble," Aidan said as he came up next to her. They walked for a long time without saying anything. Each of them lost in their own thoughts, their own problems.

"Why haven't you left yet?" Falon asked breaking the long silence. The attraction she was feeling for him was disturbing her. She'd never been so drawn to someone before. It would be best for him to leave. It would be better for both of them. Aidan looked down at Falon as they came to the edge of a small stream, and she sat down. He thought for a moment, debating on telling her that they were mates, but he figured she would not be ready to hear that just yet. "Cale, has formed an attachment with Ariana."

Falon looked at the stream instead of looking at Aidan. "Does that mean that you two won't be going anywhere?"

"Yes," Aidan said as he leaned his shoulder against a tree. He looked down at Falon. She really was beautiful with her red hair falling about her shoulders. It reminded him of fire. Aidan looked away as a old memory surfaced. A long time ago when the Elementals ruled he had been told that his mate would be a different kind of Fire Elemental. A special one, a strong one. It had been hard to take considering the Elementals were all bad. Of course, in the end it had not mattered. He'd been one of the ones to help wipe them all out giving up his chance of ever finding his mate. Aidan looked back down at Falon and a peace settled in him like he had never known before. He had been given a second chance and he was not going to waste it. He was going to stay with Falon and protect her. Nothing was going to come between him and his mate. Nothing was going to take her away from him.

Falon stood up and dusted off her pants. Aidan raised an eyebrow as he looked her up and down. Man, she was gorgeous. She may be stubborn and annoying, but she was nice to look at. "Is that a problem?" Aidan asked getting back on topic.

Falon sighed and rubbed the back of her neck. "It may be. Ariana and I don't exactly live alone. Those we live with may not be too thrilled about you two coming home with us."

Aidan's chest tightened as thoughts of Falon with another man went through his mind. The idea that she was already taken had not entered his mind at all. Well whom ever she was with was going to have a fight on his hands, because she was his and he would be second to no one. "Cale will be upset about that," he said his voice tense and tight. He didn't like the idea of another man touching her. Dammit, he was the only man who had the right to touch her! She was his! When had he become so possessive? Aidan shook his head and almost laughed at his on possessiveness.

Falon looked at Aidan in confusion, "why would he be upset? He is not the one who is bringing two Fae bounty hunters home. I'm going to be in so much trouble." Her energy was fading, and she knew she needed to get some rest. She looked at him then headed back to the cave.

91

"He would be upset because he believes that no one has any claim on Ariana. I'm sure both of your lovers won't be happy with you bringing two men home," Aidan said his fist clenched. Falon stopped and then burst out laughing. "What is so funny?" Aidan asked not finding anything about this situation amusing. The thought of Falon in another man's arms was angering him.

"One, Cale has nothing to worry about. Ariana has no lovers," Falon said taking deep breaths trying not to burst out laughing again, but she could not help it. "And two.." She said between her laughs, "who in their right mind would be mine? As you have pointed out I don't use my head, and I'm a tad crazy." Falon put her hands on her knees and was finally able to stop laughing.

Aidan tilted his head and looked at her. She was serious. She really thought that no man would want to be with her. "With the way you act I would think your self confidence would be greater than it is. I'm sure that there are lots of men who want to be with you," Aidan said the tightness in his chest lessening. He didn't have any lovers to kill, but he did have to work on her confidence.

Falon scoffed, but said nothing. When they came closer to the caves she stopped and turned to Aidan with a serious expression on her face, "Ariana is my best friend and my family if Cale hurts her in any way I'll kill him."

Aidan should have been taken aback by her tone and the seriousness of what she said, but he wasn't. "Cale is a good man, and he wouldn't hurt Ariana," Aidan said trying to reassure Falon.

Falon looked away trying to hide the sadness that came into her eyes. As Aidan saw the sadness he wanted to do everything in his power to take it away. "There have been many good men who have tried to slit my throat, Aidan. Trust doesn't come easily for me. I'm telling you this out of consideration. If he hurts her I won't hesitate to kill him."

Aidan looked down at her, "I would never allow him to hurt her, but you don't have to worry." Falon gave him an annoyed look, "How could someone so young become so cynical about others?"

Falon wanted to be angry at the question, but she knew what he said was true. Instead of looking at him she looked towards the woods, "I have lived through a lot in my short years, and I have learned two things." Falon ran her hand through her hair, "never let your guard down and be careful who you trust." Falon went to walk away, but Aidan grabbed her wrist to stop her. Falon looked down at his hand and instead of feeling the normal panic about someone touching her she felt warmth.

"What happened to you?" Aidan asked as he brought up his other hand and brushed a piece of hair out of her face. "Who hurt you so bad that you don't trust?" His voice was soft and gentle. Whoever it was he was going to kill them with his bare hands.

Falon gently moved away from him and looked at him with a mixture of pain and shame. "We should get some rest. We have a long walk ahead of us tomorrow." With that she went back into the caves. Aidan shook his head and followed after her.

Chapter Five

"You're lost," Aidan said accusingly. He looked around and saw a tree that he could have sworn he saw two hours ago.

"I'm not lost," Falon mumbled as she pushed her way through another bush. Okay, so maybe she was lost, but she would die before she admitted that to him. Somehow they had gotten separated from the rest of the group, and now they were lost.

"Falon, why don't you just admit it. You have no idea where we are," Aidan remarked as he followed after the stubborn woman in front of him. Well, at least he was getting a nice view of her backside. Aidan shook his head and told himself to focus. It was never a good thing to be lost in the woods.

"I know exactly where we are, and you didn't have to come after me. I can take care of myself," Falon snapped.

Aidan scoffed, "I have yet to see that."

Falon whipped around, "Who saved your life in the bar?! And who took out those Witches there?! Just because I have had a...a...little bad luck doesn't mean that I can't take care of myself! And if you want to know something, my bad luck started when I met you." She then turned around and stomped off.

Aidan shook his head and hurried to catch up with her. "I'm not bad luck!" he yelled as he pushed a limb aside so she could go through. He didn't like the idea of her thinking he was bad luck.

Falon looked over at him then gave him a small smile, "I know." Falon suddenly stopped causing Aidan to run into her back. She put her arm out to steady him then she listened careful. Falon cursed under her breath, then she pulled Aidan down into some bushes. "What.." Before he could say more she had rolled on top of him and covered his mouth with her hand. Aidan started to listen and that's when he heard someone talking. He looked up to see Falon looking down at him. When he nodded she took her hand away from his mouth. How could he have not known there were people near? Aidan looked up and he knew how he could have messed that. The woman that was on top of him had taken all of his focus away. Even now with her on top of him he couldn't focus. All he could think about was pulling her down for a kiss.

Falon tried to roll off of Aidan but he held her in place with his hands on her hips. She looked down at him and tilted her head in confusion. Of course, the confusion was quickly replaced with something she couldn't explain when his hands moved up her body. Aidan's hand cupped the back of her neck bringing her down to him. Before she could even protest his lips were capturing hers in a kiss. She wanted to resist, but she couldn't. She just couldn't find the will to fight him. Instead she braced her hands on his shoulders and enjoyed the kiss. She found some of her sense and was about to pull back when he used his thumb to apply pressure to her chin to open her mouth. Once she opened her mouth to him she was lost as his tongue invaded her mouth and the kiss deepened. Falon closed her eyes as she let herself enjoy what Aidan was doing to her. It just felt so right to be in his arms. It felt right to be kissing him like this.

Aidan quickly rolled Falon onto her back as the kiss deepened. He was just starting to move his hand down her body when he heard a twig snap. Suddenly, everything was brought back into focus. They were supposed to be hiding and being quiet. What had he been thinking kissing her when danger was near? He would never forgive himself if something happened to her because of his stupidity and lack of control.

Falon stilled and looked up at Aidan with a startled look. They both stayed as still as possible as the footsteps came closer. "I know I heard something," A man's voice rang out. Falon stiffened as she recognized the voice. Aidan looked at Falon with a quizzical look as he felt her stiffen under him.

"Come on we need to get going," Another voice said, this one even closer to Aidan and Falon's hiding place. "Damian won't be happy if we're late." At the mention of Damian Aidan stiffened and it was Falon's turn to look at him questioningly. When Falon looked into Aidan's eyes he looked worried. He almost looked unsure of himself. Since Falon had met him he had always put off an air of confidence it was one of the things that she liked about him. It was as if nothing could bother him but right now the mention of Damian was making him looked worried. Of course, everyone had a reason to be worried when it came to Damian. *That crazy Fae,* Falon thought as she rubbed Aidan's arm. When he touched her she always felt safe and at peace. Maybe she could give him some of that by touching him.

Aidan looked into Falon's eyes and wondered how she would see him if she knew the truth. Would she forgive him for it? Those thoughts were running through his mind until she rubbed his arm. As she touched him all he felt was the warmth that she brought when she was near. Suddenly, he knew that everything was going to be all right. He just had to hang on to her tightly and never let her go. No matter what happened everything would be all right as long as he had her.

Falon knew they were running out of time. Quietly she said an incantation that would make a sound come from the opposite direction they were in. Once they left it would only be a matter of seconds before they realized that it had been a trick.

"Over there," one of the men said in a shout and they both ran off. Aidan quickly got up, pulled Falon to her feet, and the two took off running in the opposite direction. As they ran they heard shouts behind them but neither slowed down or looked back. Of course, as their luck would have it their journey came to a sudden end as they slid to a halt at the edge of a cliff. "Is Fate working against us?" Falon asked as she looked over the edge of the cliff. She shook her head then turned to face the woods. It looked like they would be fighting. As she listened she realized that the two men had been joined by others.

"This day just keeps getting better and better," Aidan said as he looked down and saw the river below them. He turned to hear more men coming towards them. Aidan took a deep breath and got himself ready for a battle. He would protect Falon even if it killed him.

Falon looked over her shoulder. She knew the men were not far behind, and she was not going to get caught. Falon looked over her shoulder one more time ,and she knew what she needed to do. She looked at Aidan and hoped he would forgive her for what she was about to do. "Aidan, I'm sorry," she said as their eyes met.

Aidan looked at Falon and saw the worry and fear in her eyes. He didn't like it. Aidan was about to ask her why she was sorry when she knocked him off the cliff. As they fell his only thought was if they survived this he was going to kill her.

Falon hit the cold, icy water and lost her breath. As she went under the water and was swept away by the current the only thing she could think about was getting to Aidan. As she fought the current and tried to make it to shore she hoped that Aidan was all right. She would never forgive herself if she had just gotten him killed. After fighting the current for what seemed like hours she finally made it to shore. She pulled herself out of the water and fell into an exhausted heap. Falon wanted to lie there until she caught her breath but Fate had other plans. As she looked up she saw two sets of boots in front of her. She heard a maniacal laugh, then she was grabbed by the head of her hair. "Let me go, you giant oaf," Falon spat out as she grabbed his wrist.

"You're a fiery thing," The Fae said as he jerked her to her feet and pulled her close to him. "You'll be a lot of fun."

Falon's eyes turned red, but she held back. It would be a bad thing if she lost control. Carefully Falon pulled some power from her Witch's Stone and threw the large Fae away from her. She stood on shaky legs and faced the two Fae. "Let's play," she said with an evil glare as she pulled out her knife. She fought with everything in her bringing forward power that she tried to keep under control.

When the fight ended she fell to her knees out of breath. Falon looked over at the Fae and shook her head. "Fools," she said to their dead bodies. She had tried to not kill them but they wouldn't stop coming at her. In the end she had no choice. Falon shook her head, got to her feet, and headed away from the bodies. She needed to find Aidan. As long as Aidan was all right then what she had done would be worth it. A shiver ran down Falon's spine as the fight replayed itself in her head. A blast here, a slash with her knife there, but it was the final burst of power, the power that she tried not to use, that had been the death blow. Falon's shoulders slumped as she realized she would never be a normal Human. She was always going to be a monster.

~~~

Falon had been looking for Aidan for over an hour with no luck. She rounded another bend in the river and saw a body laying face down in the mud. "Aidan!" she yelled as she ran towards the body. With her hands shaking she rolled him over onto his back. "I've killed him," she screamed out as panic started to take hold of her. If she hadn't been so concerned about her own well fair then Aidan would not be lying here. Falon gently brushed his hair out of his face and cringed when she saw the large cut on his forehead. She placed her shaking hand on his chest, and was relieved when she felt his chest rise and fall. "Thank goodness. Okay, don't worry I'm going to fix you right up," Falon said as she got control of herself. She knew that what she was about to do would take a lot of her strength, but she had to do it. She had to save Aidan. She pushed her energy into Aidan and felt him begin to heal. She had him almost completely healed when she heard a laugh behind her.

"Well, well. I thought we'd lost you."

"Really! I can't catch a break," Falon exclaimed with a frustrated tone. She slowly stood up and turned to see one of the first men who had been chasing her and Aidan. She placed herself in between the man and Aidan. She hadn't just healed Aidan for him to get hurt in some cross fire.

Falon used as much power as she could and threw it at the man knocking him out cold. She knew she shouldn't have used that much power especially after healing Aidan, but she was so tired of all of this. Falon fell to her knees, her breathing became ragged and labored as she felt her energy began to fade. She shook her head and forced herself to her feet once again. She knew that until she had Aidan safely away from all of the Fae she wouldn't be able to rest. Falon went over to Aidan and with everything in her she started to drag him away. She just hoped she didn't cause anymore damage.

~~~

Aidan woke up as his leg hit a stone. He felt strange. It was as if someone was dragging him. He slowly opened his eyes to see Falon above him. "Falon?" he asked softly. His mind becoming even more confused than before.

104

Falon jumped and let go of Aidan as she heard him speak. When he hit the ground she winced. "Sorry," she said sympathetically as she dropped to her knees next to him. "Are you all right?" she asked as she looked him over. "I didn't hurt you did I?"

"I'm fine. What happened? I remember you pushing me off the cliff but after that things get hazy," Aidan said as he slowly sat up. He'd been expecting some kind of pain but there was none. Actually, he felt better than he had in a long time. Aidan shook his head not understanding why he felt so good.

"I'm so sorry. I almost killed you," Falon said as she launched herself into his arms. "I thought you were dead when I found you."

Aidan's arms wrapped around Falon, and he felt her body shaking. "I'm fine," Aidan looked around trying to get his bearings. "Falon, where are we?" he asked as she pulled back from him.

"I don't know. I...I have just been trying..." Falon shook her head as tiredness swept over her. She needed to stay awake for a little while longer, "to get you to safety. I made my way to

the shore then I was attacked. After dealing
with that I found you unconscious...I helped
you then another Fae showed up."

Aidan jerked his head back to her, and he
grabbed her by the shoulders to make her focus
on him. "Were you hurt? Did they hurt you?"
He looked at her and saw the dark circles under
her eyes. She looked horrible. "Answer me!"
Aidan yelled when Falon didn't say anything.

"No, but I used a lot of power. I've been
dragging you for the past two hours, while
covering up our tracks." Falon blinked her eyes
a couple of times, but it was no good. She was
just so tired. "I'm just...so tired," Falon said
slowly then everything went black.

Aidan quickly grabbed her to keep her from
hitting her face on the ground. He moved her
to her back and cradled her in his arms. "Falon?
Falon, wake up," Aidan said as he shook her a
little. He placed his hand on her chest and felt it
rise and fall. She was all right, just exhausted.
"Rest. I'll look out for you, my mate." He gently
laid her on the ground. Aidan saw her shiver.
He knew that she needed out of those wet
clothes before she became sick. He looked at
his clothes and realized he needed to as well. He

used his magic to quickly change his clothes then he changed hers. After that he scooped her up in his arms and began looking for a place for them to stay the night. Somewhere safe where he could keep an eye on her. He should have been the one to save her. Aidan shook his head as he realized that nothing was what he thought it was with her. Every idea he ever had about what his mate would be like was thrown out the window when he met her. Of course, he wouldn't have it any other way.

Chapter Six

Falon opened her eyes and slowly sat up. She looked around and noticed that she was in a cave with a fire going nearby. Once she got over the shock of waking somewhere different she realized she was in different clothes. Falon looked down at her clothes and laughed.

"Well I see you're awake. You had me worried. You have been out for four hours," Aidan said as he came into the cave carrying wood in his arms.

"I don't know if I'm awake or not. I'm pretty sure that when I...." She didn't want to say passed out because it made her seem weak, "fell asleep I was not wearing this dress," Falon said with a raised eyebrow.

Aidan looked Falon up and down taking in her body in the dress. The dress was cut low, tight to her body, and made her brown eyes pop. Aidan shrugged, "Your other clothes were too wet, so I had to make you something else," he said without a hint of apology. Although for the past four hours he had been worrying about her, he had also been enjoying the way she looked in that dress. Okay, thinking that through made him sound really bad. Actually, it made him sound really creepy. Oh well, she was his mate. If he wanted to enjoy looking at her that was his business but no one else was going to get that privilege. Wow, there was that possessiveness again. Aidan shrugged and placed the wood next to the fire.

"And you couldn't have put me in pants or I don't know something that isn't so low or..." Falon looked at him with a smirk, "tight."

Aidan came over with the sexiest smile she'd ever seen. "I think you look amazing," he said, his voice taking on a husky tone. He wanted to kiss her until she wasn't thinking about what she was wearing but only him. *All right get your head screwed on straight. You need to behave,* Aidan thought to himself. She needed to know a few things about him before they were together in every way.

"Yes, well it is impossible to travel with something like this on," Falon looked towards the fire. She closed her eyes and drank in the energy of it. She was still tired, and she needed more rest, but she also wanted to talk to Aidan. "I'm sorry," she said softly.

"For what?"

"I pushed you off a cliff, you got hurt, and....we're lost," she said with a depressed voice. She pulled her knees up to her chest and wrapped her arms around them. "I promise I'm usually not this incompetent," Falon sighed sadly. "I can understand why you think so little of me."

Aidan shook his head and chuckled, "You aren't incompetent, and I don't think little of you. Actually, I think very highly of you."

Falon looked at Aidan with her eyebrows scrunched. "Really, why?"

"Because you are strong and brave. You stand up to me," Aidan sighed and rubbed the back of his neck. "I'll admit that I didn't like being pushed off a cliff, but I understand why you did it. If they would have caught us things would have gotten ugly. However, I do wish you would think things through more. You are going to be the death of me if you don't," Aidan said with a smile as he looked at Falon. His heart melted as a true smile spread across her face. It was the first real smile she had given him.

"I'll work on that," Falon said then looked back at the fire. "So do you think we need to move tonight or wait until morning?"

"Morning, I have put some protection around us, so no one will be able to find us. That way, we can get a good nights sleep and be ready to find our way to your home in the morning." Aidan leaned against the cave wall, closed his eyes, and crossed his legs at the ankles. "You know if you told me where we were going I could help you find it."

"I can't do that," Falon said as she put her head on her knees and looked over at him. She looked him over enjoying the view. She was just bringing her eyes back to his face when she noticed that he was staring at her. She quickly turned her face away blushing. It was just her luck that he would catch her sneaking looks at him. Oh well, she had never been a subtle person. Falon sighed and tried to understand what Aidan was doing to her. She couldn't explain the pull he had over her or the way he made her feel. She'd never had this problem before. Falon had always been able to maintain her distance, so why couldn't she with Aidan.

Aidan watched as Falon blushed and look away from him. She really was beautiful. He was about to say something when he saw her shiver, "come here."

"What?" Falon asked as she looked back over at Aidan.

"Come here," he said again, softly. Aidan leaned forward wrapped one arm around her waist then pulled her against his side. It felt so right to have her next to him with his arm around her waist. "You're cold."

Falon felt heat shoot through her body, "ummm...I don't think..." But before she could finish he'd grabbed her chin and tilted her face toward his. He leaned down and kissed her. As the kiss deepened Aidan moved her so that he could push her to her back. Aidan groaned as his body came down on top of hers. Falon felt like she was on fire as his hand moved down her body. She moaned as he left her mouth and kissed her neck. "Aidan..," She said breathlessly as his hand brushed her sides. "We can't do this."

Aidan stopped kissing Falon's neck and sighed. She was right. He knew she was right. Before they could do this he had to tell her the truth, because once they were together in every way she would be his and only his. She deserved the truth. "You're right. I shouldn't have started this. I'm..." Before he could apologize she covered his mouth with her hand.

"If you apologize I'll kick you," she said with a sparkle in her eyes.

Aidan nodded his head and kissed her palm. She removed her hand, and he brushed some hair out of her face. "Let's get some sleep," he rolled off of her, but before she could move away he pulled her back against his chest. "It will help us stay warm if we are next to each other."

Falon knew that it was a bad idea, she knew she didn't need to get too close, but as his chin rested on her head and his arm wrapped around her waist she couldn't fight it. She was in deep trouble.

~~~

Falon woke up with her dress raised to the middle of her thigh. Her head was on Aidan's chest and her hand was resting on his stomach. One of her legs draped across his. She slowly tried to sit up, to put some distance between them, but as she moved his arm tightened around her waist, and he mumbled something in his sleep. Falon swore as she looked down and saw her dress rise higher. Finally, she was able to move her leg off of Aidan and use her hand to pull down her dress a little, but not enough for her to be comfortable.

"What are you doing?" Aidan asked without opening his eyes.

"Trying to get up," Falon said quietly.

"But I'm not ready to get up," Aidan said as he opened his eyes and looked into Falon's. His eyes moved down her body until they landed on her exposed legs. Aidan's sleepiness faded as he saw her exposed legs. Putting her in that dress was not the best idea he had ever had. Well part of him thought that, the other part was like hell yes, this was the best idea in the world. It was that part that was starting to take control.

Falon's face flushed as she realized he was looking at her legs, "Well you don't have to, but I need to get up." She attempted to move out of his arms, but he tightened his hold, rolled her onto her back, and secured her with his body.

"But I won't rest if you are not next to me," he said his eyes showing the passion he was feeling. Yeah, now your lying to yourself. *You know you don't want to rest,* he thinks to himself as he looks into her beautiful eyes.

Falon took in a lung full of air. She swore she forgot to breath. "Aidan..." She couldn't get anything out as she felt his hand move to her leg. "We...need," but she was silenced as his lips came down on hers. She felt the fire building in her that only Aidan could start, and she didn't understand it. Falon's brain shut down as Aidan's hand pushed up her dress a little further. Everywhere he touched seemed to be on fire. Falon wrapped her arms around his neck bringing him even closer to her.

Aidan knew they needed to stop. He couldn't finish this. He knew this, but as Falon wrapped her arms around his neck he forgot all about his good intentions. Aidan moved his body, so that it was completely on top of Falon, then he moved his hand so it was brushing against her side and breast. He pulled back from the kiss long enough to untie the laces on the bodice of Falon's dress. Aidan wanted to touch her so badly that he couldn't stop. He was almost done when Falon grabbed his hand.

"We can't do this, Aidan. I can't do this," Falon said her voice coming out in a raspy whisper. What was happening to her? She used to have control until Aidan came into her life. Now all he had to do was look at her, and she lost her control completely.

Her words pulled Aidan back to the present. He swore under his breath and pulled away from her. He sat up and ran his hand through his hair. "I-" Aidan started, but before he could say anything else Falon stood up and walked out of the cave. Aidan put his head in his hands. What was wrong with him? He had never been this out of control before.

Aidan pulled himself together and grabbed their belongings. He was sure Falon would be back in a few minutes. He looked to where she had gone and sighed. "I'll give her a few minutes then I'm going after her."

Falon kept walking after she left the cave. She felt the tears fill her eyes as words she had been called since she was a child filled her mind. "What was I thinking?" She wiped at the tears that fell down her cheek. She always thought that she wasn't what all those men said, but maybe she was. Falon refused to admit the reason she had allowed Aidan such liberties was because she cared for him. She stopped dead in her tracks as her thoughts caught up with her. She felt her knees go weak as she thought it through some more. She did care for him. She cared for that stubborn, obnoxious Fae. How the hell did that happen?

Falon shook her head and kept walking, her mind racing. She didn't know where she was going, and she didn't care. Right now all she knew was she needed to get away and clear her head. She needed to get Aidan out of her mind. She couldn't care for him. This was ridiculous.

~~~

117

Aidan waited for Falon to return, but she never did. He swore under his breath and left the caves. Apparently, she wasn't trying to hide from him because she didn't cover her tracks.

Aidan quickly followed her tracks hoping he could get to her before something happened to her. He should have gone after her as soon as she left. He should have made her tell him why she didn't want to be with him. Aidan shook his head as he realized he shouldn't have let her go. "How can one woman move so fast?" Aidan asked, as he followed the tracks.

In the past three hours, he had thought he was close to catching up with her, but the tracks continued on. "No," Aidan yelled out once he lost her tracks. He ran his hand through his hair in frustration as he tried to figure out what to do.

Falon's voice rang out from the trees. "Aidan, get out of there!"

Aidan looked up to see Falon high in the tree next to him. "What-Falon get down!" Before he could say anything else his attention was drawn to a very, very large animal coming toward him. He used his abilities to send a blast at the beast, but it just pissed off the animal more. He was about to attack again when the animal hit him, knocking him against the tree.

Aidan hit the ground, trying to catch his breath, but found it impossible. He knew he needed to get up and fight but the pain was too bad.

"Get away from him!" Falon yelled as she jumped down in front of Aidan. She had to protect him. It was her fault he was in this mess. If she would have handled the situation like an adult instead of running away, this wouldn't have happened.

"Falon, run!" Aidan said, his voice showing his pain. He knew that he didn't have much time left. "Falon, please run." He tried to get to his feet. He had to make sure she was all right. If that was all he had left in him he would make sure that she lived.

Falon looked over at Aidan and saw the paleness of his face. "Don't move. I'll take care of this thing." She turned her attention to the beast that was getting ready to charge again. Saying an incantation, she threw a bolt of power toward the beast. She cringed when it did nothing to the creature. "Great. Of course, you're immune to magic." She began to frantically looked around for a means to get the animal to leave them alone.

Falon slowly moved until her back was to a tree and waited. "This is going to hurt if I don't time it right." As the beast charged, Falon waited until the last possible moment and dived to her left. She quickly regained her feet and smirked as the beast rammed into the tree.

She watched as the animal shook its head and looked at her. As the animal got ready to charge again, Falon put her back to yet another tree. "Come on. Come on!" she screamed as it charged once again.

Aidan watched as Falon held her place again. Three times he watched as the beast charged his mate and each time he felt his heart drop to his stomach. Finally, the beast shook his head and gave up. Falon came over to him and knelt next to him.

Falon saw the blood coming out of Aidan's mouth and knew that she was running out of time. As she placed her hands on his chest she knew that if she did this, she would be pushing her powers to their limit. There was a possibility that by saving him, she would be forfeiting her life for his.

Falon touched his face with her fingers. "Everything will be all right. I promise," she said more emotion filling her than ever before. She couldn't watch him die.

Aidan leaned into Falon's touch. He hungered to feel it, just one more time. He tried to say something to her, anything, but before he could everything went black.

Pain began to radiate through her whole body as she pushed power into Aidan. Falon continued to push her power through Aidan until she knew that he was healed. When she felt his chest rise and fall in a normal manner, she allowed the darkness to consume her. She passed out with her head on Aidan's chest and a peace in knowing that Aidan was going to be all right.

Chapter Seven

Aidan woke with a pounding headache. As he looked up at the sky, he saw that the sun was almost fully gone. He became confused as he went through his last memories. They were all jumbled, but when he finally got a grip on them, panic began to sink in. It had been at least five hours since he had passed out and the last thing he remembered was Falon speaking to him.

At the thought of Falon, a different type of panic filled him. Where was she? Where was his mate? He called her name as he looked around. As he tried to sit up, he felt something on his chest.

"Falon, wake up." He shook her gently, worry clenched his heart as she laid there, lifeless, on top of him.

He tried to hold her steady as he sat up so that she wouldn't fall to the ground. "Please, wake up." He cradled her in his arms. "Don't do this to me, sweetheart. Don't leave me," he said softly as he moved his shaking hand to Falon's chest. He let out a relieved sigh as he felt her chest rise and fall. She was breathing, weakly, but she was breathing.

Aidan put his forehead to Falon's. "You have to stop doing this to me." Aidan gently stood up with her in his arms and looked at the sky as thunder sounded in the distance. "I'll keep you safe. Just don't leave me."

After finding a dry cave he laid her down on the ground and brushed a lock of hair out of her face. "You're going to be all right," he said as he leaned down and kissed her gently on the lips. When he pulled back he saw a slow smile spread across her face. It was there for only a moment, but it had been there.

Aidan chuckled. "So you do enjoy my touch," he said as he played with her hair. "If you enjoy my touch then why do you always pull back and want me to stop?" He knew he wouldn't get an answer, but it was something that had been bothering him.

Aidan ran his finger down her face until it ran across her lower lip. He smiled when a little sigh escaped her lips. "I'll figure you out. I promise you." He placed one more kiss on her lips. He pulled back and looked at the fire. She was going to be all right. He wasn't going to lose her. Not yet, not ever. She was going to be his. Forever.

~~~

Falon woke up feeling like she had been run over by the beast she had tried to get away from. Maybe it had hit her, maybe that was why she felt so crummy. She closed her eyes trying to get her memories to not be so jumbled, so she could remember what had happened. Finally, it all came together. "Aidan," Falon called out her voice sounding weak and raspy.

"I thought you'd never wake up," Aidan said as he came over and sat down next to her. He saw the dark circles under her eyes and the pale look of her skin. "Are you okay?" he asked, the worry evident in his voice.

"I'll be fine. How long have I been out?"

"Close to a day," Aidan said as he brushed her cheek gently with the back of his hand.

Falon closed her eyes and groaned. She then tried to sit up.

"No stay still. You need to rest more." It had been torture waiting for her to wake up. During his waiting, he had realized that he was beginning to care for her. Actually care and that scared him to death. What if he suddenly started to care, and he lost her? Aidan scrunched his eyebrows together as he wondered if she cared for him.

"Aidan, I need to get up and-" Falon blushed. "See to some things. I'll rest some more when I get back," she said her eyebrows scrunching together.

Aidan kissed her on the forehead then helped her stand up. "You'll be right back?" he asked, as he brushed a piece of hair out of her face.

"I'll be right back," she said giving him a small smile.

~ ~ ~

125

Aidan woke up and smiled at the woman laying next to him. He could definitely get use to this. Waking up with Falon in his arms was the most amazing feeling he had ever felt before.

"Why are you staring at me?" Falon asked in a sleepy voice without opening up her eyes.

"I-" Aidan stumbled trying to come up with a good enough lie to tell her but nothing came to mind. "How did you know that I was staring at you?" *Yeah good going change the subject.*

"I could feel it." Falon turned over so that she could look at Aidan, "I think we should get going."

Aidan sighed heavily. "Do you know where we are?" He raised an eyebrow as he watched Falon chew on her bottom lip.

Falon finally lowered her eyes so that she was looking at Aidan's chest. "No." She then took a deep breath. "We are trying to get to Crook's Mountain," she said softly as she brought her eyes back to Aidan's. She was waiting for him to call her stupid or make fun because she couldn't find her own home, but instead he just smiled down sweetly at her.

Aidan cupped the side of her face with his hand. "See nothing bad happened when you told me."

Falon scrunched her face at him making Aidan laugh.

"Come on," Aidan said as he stood up and held out his hand for Falon.

Falon quickly grabbed his hand.

"So how hard was it for you to tell me?" Aidan asked as he watched with great interest as Falon bent over to pick up her bag.

"Very hard. I'm not use to...well to needing help. Do you think you know how to get us from wherever we are to Crook's Mountain?" Falon asked, she looked over her shoulder at Aidan. She smirked when she caught him looking at her butt. "My eyes are up here."

Aidan cleared his throat and looked away trying to hide the embarrassment of getting caught looking at Falon's backside. "Yes, I know how to get us there. Actually, we're only about two hours away I believe."

"Thank goodness. I'm ready to be home. I could do with a hot bath," Falon said as she left the cave.

Aidan shook his head trying to get his mind clear of the image that had just came into it. "So why are we going to Crook's Mountain? Is that where Cale and the others will meet up with us?" Aidan asked as he looked away from Falon. Looking at her was only aiding his mind into picturing her in a bath.

"Well, yes, considering that is our destination. My home is kind of built in the mountain." Falon started to walk past Aidan when he grabbed her by the arm.

"Your home is what?" he asked in shock. He must have misunderstood her. There was nothing built in the mountain. It was just a plain mountain. Nothing special about it.

"My home is built in Crook's Mountain," Falon said giving him a charming smile. "Surprised?"

"Very," Aidan said with a smile then he quickly pulled Falon into his arms. "Are you sure that your sense of direction isn't bad because you are heading to the wrong place?" he asked with a crocked smile.

Falon laughed. "No, I promise that Crook's Mountain is where we are going, and just so you know, I usually have a very good sense of direction. I have just been more distracted than normal, and it caused me to not pay close enough attention," Falon said as she looked away from Aidan.

Falon cursed herself as she felt her face flush with embarrassment. Why had she just told him that? Nothing good could come out of playing this game. She needed to go back to this all being a beautiful lie instead of her trying to make it a truth. A reality.

Aidan grabbed Falon's chin with his hand and turned her face so she was looking at him. "And what had you so distracted?" he asked his voice growing husky and sexy as he moved his face closer to Falon's. He wanted so bad to touch her. To taste her. Just thinking about it had his heart rate speeding up, and his blood feeling like it was on fire.

"I...um...have no idea," Falon said with a mischievous smile. She was not giving in to him that easily. She mentally kicked herself. She was flirting. Why was she flirting? *All right you stop right this minute.* Falon told herself, but it was all for nothing.

"Are you sure?" Aidan asked right before his mouth covered her's. Aidan wrapped his arms around Falon's waist and pulled her tight against him.

Falon couldn't think as Aidan kissed her. All she could do was feel. What was it about this man that made her lose all her thoughts? Falon felt like she was on fire. She couldn't help herself when she wrapped her arms around his neck. Being in Aidan's arms seemed so right. Falon moaned as Aidan's lips left her's, and he began to kiss and nibble at her neck. "Aidan, we need to...," Falon lost her train of thought has Aidan's hands began to move over her body. Dear night this felt so good. So right.

Aidan finally made himself stop and pull back. He put his forehead against Falon's and tried to get his heart to slow down. "So why have you been so distracted lately?" he asked his voice coming out sounding out of breath.

Aidan knew he had her when she closed her eyes.

Falon closed her eyes trying to get her heartbeat to slow down. As fast as it was beating she very much feared it was going to explode. "I may know why I've been distracted. And it may or may not have something to do with you," she said quietly as she laid her head against Aidan's chest. "Aidan...I...," Falon cleared her throat, shook her head to clear it from the spell he weaved over her, and took a step back. When her eyes met his she felt like her heart was breaking. He deserved better than her. "It isn't safe with me. Maybe you should-" But before she could finish Aidan had grabbed a hold of her and kissed her again. When he pulled back he cupped the sides of her face.

"I'm not going anywhere. Besides, I haven't had this much of an adventure in a long time," Aidan said with a charming smile. *Please don't push me away,* Aidan thought to himself.

"Yes, because almost dying several times is loads of fun," Falon said sarcastically as she ran her hand through her hair in frustration. This was ridiculous. Nothing could ever happen between them. Once he learned about her he would leave. What then? What would happen to her? She knew what would happen. She would be left alone trying to pick up the pieces of her broken heart, because if anyone could get to her heart it was him. And, boy, was he close to it already.

Falon took a deep breath as the other part of her mind woke up. Why couldn't she enjoy him? For just a little while. If he left then at least she would have the memories to keep her company. Falon shook her head she was starting to sound like she had a split personality. Aidan was really driving her crazy, and he didn't even know it. Ever since she met him she didn't even know her own thoughts.

"Which way?" Falon asked her voice taking on a depressed tone to it.

"I'll tell you if you'll listen to me," Aidan said as he grabbed her hand in his. "I'm not going anywhere, and I have enjoyed being with you. Actually, this is the most fun I've had in a very long time."

Falon looked back at Aidan then looked at their hands. "Thank you," she said as she gave him a hesitant smile. "It has been the most fun

I've had as well. Well, excluding the almost dying parts."

Aidan laughed then put his arm around her shoulders. "Yes, I could have done without that as well. Hey, I've been meaning to ask. What incantation do you use to heal people? I know there are some, but I thought the knowledge was lost," Aidan asked as he turned her in the direction they were going and the two took off walking.

It was the truth he had been curious about how she saved him, but really he just wanted to change the topic. He was worried that she was going to tell him that he would be better without her. His gut tightened just thinking about being apart from her. Somehow he was going to have to convince her that he meant to stay, that they were meant to be together. Soon he would tell her everything. He would tell her she was his mate and everything would be all right.

Falon shrugged off his arm then hurried ahead. "Come on. I'm ready for a good meal and a hot bath," she said quickly, avoiding answering the question. She had finally made up her mind to enjoy her time with Aidan, and she wasn't going to ruin it by telling him the truth just now, later she would tell him. Yes, she would tell him the truth later. Much later if she had her way.

She left the truth about her past for later, right now she needed to worry about finding her friend, home, and how her family was going to react to Aidan. Yes, she had enough to worry about without adding telling Aidan the truth right now. She would just believe in this beautiful lie for a while longer.

~~~

Aidan pulled Falon behind a tree and covered her mouth with his hand. "I heard something," he said quietly against her ear as he pinned her to the tree with his body.

Falon raised her hand and grabbed his wrist pulling his hand away from her mouth. "That was your excuse four trees ago," she said with a raised eyebrow as she looked at Aidan's face.

Aidan gave her a crooked smile as he leaned down so that their lips were almost touching. "I'm just being cautious." Aidan took in her scent and how she look. Man she was amazing.

"Yeah right," Falon said as she cupped the back of his neck with her hand and pulled his head the rest of the way down.

Aidan placed his hands on either side of her head against the tree as he deepened the kiss. This two hour trip had turned into a three almost four hour trip because he kept stopping and finding reasons to kiss Falon. To stir up the passion that he knew was in her. *Oh well, it was definitely worth it,* he thought to himself as Falon's hands moved up under his shirt.

Aidan ran his hands down her arms, and finally, he wrapped them around her waist pulling her close to him. He was just thinking about lowering them both to the ground when Falon tensed.

"What's wrong?" Aidan asked as she turned her head away from him. He knew something was wrong by the way she had tensed.

"We're not alone," Falon said as she moved her hands out from under Aidan's shirt and looked around. Falon closed her eyes to try and pin point who exactly was near.

"Damn," Aidan said under his breath. This was getting ridiculous. All he wanted was to spend some valuable time with his mate and now there was someone interrupting it. Seriously, what did a guy have to do to get some alone time. He would have to kill. That is what he was going to have to do.

Aidan hung his head for a moment then he began to look around. Aidan's frown, however, did not last long. As soon as he looked down, and saw Falon's enchanting smile spread across her face he couldn't help but smile as well.

"Ariana," Falon said as she moved away from Aidan and ran towards her friend. She had only come out from behind the tree when Ariana appeared.

"Falon!" Ariana said as she ran over and hugged her friend. "I have been looking everywhere for you. Are you all right? I was so worried."

"Yes, we both are," Falon said as she looked behind her to see Aidan coming up and clasping Cale's arm with his hand.

"Well now that we're back together we can finish up this trip," Jamie said as him and his family came over to the group.

"Yes, let's. I could use a bath and a hot meal," Falon said with a smile. She then looked at Aidan with a raised eyebrow. "And maybe a soft bed."

Aidan raised his eyebrow back understanding her meaning completely. Man, this woman was something. Aidan smiled as he thought about how much he wanted to lay on something soft, but it wasn't a bed.

"Well, it looks like you two are getting along," Cale said with a chuckle.

Aidan shrugged. "Yeah, maybe we are," he said as he got rid of his smile and cleared his throat.

"Come on let's get these girls home and-" Cale looked at him with a raised eyebrow. "And find some soft beds or at least something soft."

Aidan laughed then came up behind Falon. He gently put his hand to her lower back. "We need to get going."

Falon nodded her head. "Yeah, we should be there soon."

Aidan leaned in close so that only Falon would hear what he had to say. "I'm ready for something soft too, but it isn't a bed."

Falon blushed. "I guess we'll have to see about that," she said as she looked into Aidan's eyes and saw the spark there. Making memories for later. That was what she was doing. Falon sighed as Aidan moved his hand up the back of her shirt and touched her skin. Man, he could set her on fire by just barely touching her.

Aidan was about to say something else, but Ariana cleared her throat. "Not to interrupt this moment, but we need to get going."

Aidan cleared his throat. "Yes, I guess we need to." He reluctantly removed his hand from Falon's back and took the lead. "Let's get going."

Falon looked at Ariana and noticed the look on her face. "What?" she asked defensively. If she said one thing about her and Aidan she was going to, well, she didn't really know what she was going to do.

"Nothing," Ariana said with a huge smile as she raised her hands in mock surrender. "Come on, Falon, let's get going. I would hate to keep you from a soft bed," she said in a mocking tone as she tried really hard not to laugh.

Falon's smile faded, and she began to mumble under her breath. "Think she's so funny, needs to mind her own business."

Ariana laughed. "You, my friend, are very entertaining."

Falon looked at Ariana evilly then hurried ahead.

Aidan looked back as Ariana laughed, and he saw Falon frown. He didn't like to see her upset. He was about to do something about it when Cale spoke up.

"I love it when Ariana laughs."

"Yeah, well I don't. She's making Falon frown, which means she's laughing at my mate," Aidan said in a growl.

"Aidan, they're best friends. I'm sure they laugh at each other all the time. I know I laugh at you a lot," Cale said with a huge smile.

Aidan glared at Cale, and if looks could kill Cale would be dead right now. "How about we just focus on getting everyone home?"

"Yes let's," Falon said as she caught up with the men. They came to the bottom of the mountain a few minutes later.

"Let's climb," she said as she looked at Cale and Ariana. "You two take point. Aidan and I will go last, and between the four of us we will be able to help the others."

Everyone nodded then they started the long climb up.

Chapter Eight

"Be careful," Aidan said as he helped one of the children up onto a very large boulder. After helping the child up and handing her off to her father, Aidan looked down at Falon. He couldn't help but smile as he looked at her. Since meeting her he had found a peace and happiness that he thought he would never find.

She was the first person he had ever met who could stand toe to toe to him, and by the sparkle in her eyes, he knew that she enjoyed fighting with him as much as he enjoyed fighting with her.

Aidan's smile widened as he remembered the moments when he was able to kiss her and stir up the passion that they both felt for each other. Falon was everything he had dared to dream for. "Here give me your hand," Aidan called out as Falon made her way up the rocks.

Falon put her hand out allowing Aidan to pull her up. As he grabbed her hand, her foot slipped causing her to fall. She yelled out as she slammed against the boulder. Falon winced as pain shot through her arm.

Aidan tightened his hold on her hand. "Hang on!" he yelled as he tried to pull her up, but he was having difficulties. He felt like his heart had dropped to his feet as he tried once again to pull her up. He wasn't going to let go. *Come on you can pull her up. No problem,* he thought to himself, as he tried once again to pull her to safety.

Falon looked down and saw the fall that would kill her if Aidan lost his grip. "Please don't let me go!" Falon yelled out desperately. Of all the ways to die, this was not the way she wanted to go. She hated heights. She really did not want to die this way.

Aidan heard the fear in her voice and it tore into his heart. "I won't let you go," he said firmly as he looked down into her eyes. "I promise. I'll fall with you before I let you go." He tightened his grip and pulled until she was on top of the boulder sitting next to him.

Once he knew his hands had stopped shaking, he pulled her into his arms. He put his chin on the top of her head as he tried to sooth her. "I have you, and I'll never let you go," he said softly as he ran his hand through her hair.

Aidan took a deep breath as his heart started to slow down. He closed his eyes as he thought about how many close calls they had, had in the short time they had been together. They had only been together for two weeks, but in those two weeks he had learned that he definitely was going to have to stay on his toes for the rest of their life together.

Falon was shaking from her near miss, and she was hating herself for showing weakness. As she tried to calm down, her mind raced with what Aidan had said to her. He had said that he would never let her go, but that was exactly what he was going to do to her eventually.

Her idea of making memories began to fade as she realized that letting him close and letting him in was going to be the death of her. She wasn't for sure that once she told him the truth, and he decided to leave that she would be able to let him leave. "Thank you," she said as she moved out of his arms and stood up. "I..we

143

should get going," Falon said trying to get her mind focused on the task at hand. She could focus on what she was feeling for Aidan later.

Aidan stood up, grabbed her chin, and tilted it up so she was looking at him. "It's all right to be afraid. It's only natural."

Falon's shoulders sagged. "Fear is a weakness I can't afford. Come." She moved away from him and headed up the other rocks.

Aidan sighed deeply wondering what it was going to take to get past her defenses, her walls. Sometimes it seemed like he was getting past them. He knew that her passion for him matched his own for her, but it also seemed like every time they took one step forward they would then take two steps back.

Aidan had passed the point where he just wanted to be with her because she was his mate. Now, he wanted to be with her because he cared for her, but he just could not seem to get past the walls she put up. As they continued to climb, he watched her wondering what was going on in her head.

Falon looked over her shoulder at Aidan and wondered if she could allow herself to care for him. She wanted to, but there was so much about her that she could not tell him. So much she feared to tell him. Would he look at her the same way if he knew about her past? If he knew what she was. Falon looked back up and continue climbing until she came to an entrance to a cave.

"What took you so long?" Ariana asked as Falon came into view.

"Nothing. Come," Falon said sounding depressed. She had always been one to press on. She hid her feelings and buried them deep inside, but since meeting Aidan she couldn't do it anymore. She wanted to dream and hope for a life with him. Falon shook her head knowing it was impossible. It would always be impossible. There were just too many things that stood between them. Nothing she did was going to change who she was. Nothing was going to take away her past or make Aidan stay when he learned the truth.

"Falon, what's wrong?" Ariana asked as she put her hand on her friend's shoulder.

"Nothing," Falon lashed out. She closed her eyes and took a deep breath. "I'm sorry. Let's just go. We'll have some explaining to do once we're inside. This is going to be loads of fun," Falon said sarcastically as she started to go further in the cave.

"Falon, you won't let them hurt Cale, right?" Ariana asked desperately.

Falon stopped in her tracks. She was not one to normally swear at her friend, but she couldn't help it this time. She was tired, hurt, and upset about her feelings for Aidan. "Dammit, Ariana, what are you not telling me?! What have you seen?!" Falon asked as she grabbed Ariana by the arms and made her look at her.

Cale felt anger fill him as Falon yelled at Ariana. "Hey get away from her." He went to grab Falon, but before he could he was pinned to the wall behind him. Man, that stupid Witch's stone was powerful. "Let me go!"

"This is none of your concern so stay out of it," Falon said in an angry tone of voice. She probably should not have pinned Cale to the wall, but right now she didn't care.

Aidan came into Cale pinned to the wall angry, Ariana upset, and Falon very angry. "What is going on?" he asked as he tried to come near the girls, but before he could get too far, he was blocked by an invisible shield. "Falon?" Aidan asked the confusion evident in his voice. "Falon, what is going on?" Aidan yelled out trying to get her to answer him.

Falon turned towards James and his family. "Will you please go deeper into the cave and take those two with you? We will join you shortly."

Falon let Cale go and pulled Ariana towards the entrance of the cave, not sparing any of them a second glance.

Cale went to follow, but he hit a shield. "How is she doing this? Even with a Witch's stone, she should not be this powerful."

"I don't know, but I believe the more upset she is the more powerful she is," Aidan said as he leaned against the wall. "We need to go deeper in the cave. Falon won't hurt Ariana." He wanted Falon to let him help with whatever the problem was, but right now, apparently, she just needed to talk to Ariana. He knew once she

147

had spoken to her friend that she would come to him. He just knew it. Or at least he hoped she would.

"I'm not so sure about that. Falon is..,"

Before Cale could finish his sentence Aidan had him by the arm turning him towards him.

"Falon would never harm anyone unless she had no choice. She definitely would not hurt Ariana," he said his voice tense. He knew that Cale was just worried about his mate, but that did not give him an excuse to talk about Falon in that manner.

Cale looked at his friend and sighed. "You have fallen in love with her. Her!" he said pointing towards Falon. "I know you have no choice, that she's your mate, and I'm sorry, but how could you fall in love with her. She is dangerous, stubborn, obnoxious, annoying..."

Aidan cut him off. "You need to stop before I decided that I don't mind beating my best friend's ass. Falon is an amazing woman, and she is mine. And no one, not even you, gets to talk about what is mine," Aidan said in a growl as he let go of Cale and walked off. He needed to calm down before he did something to Cale he would regret later. Cale was his best friend, well his only friend, but he wasn't going to allow anyone to talk about Falon like that.

Cale sighed deeply then after taking one last look towards where Ariana and Falon had disappeared, he followed Aidan further into the cave.

~ ~ ~

Falon looked at Ariana and ran her hand through her hair in frustration. "What have you seen?"

"They won't accept Cale and Aidan. They will try to kill them," Ariana said as she watched her friend pace. She really should have mentioned this sooner, but she knew Falon. She knew Falon would have made sure that Cale and Aidan had left.

Falon stopped and looked at Ariana, "And you were just going to let them walk into the city. Are you crazy?! Have you lost all your senses?!"

"They are meant to be with us. And you can save them. I know you can," Ariana said as she looked into Falon's eyes. "Please, Falon."

"You are betting their lives on the hope that I can save them." Falon ran her hands down her face. "I wish I had as much faith in me as you do. Ariana," Falon said her voice losing the angry tone and becoming one of defeat, "we can't take them with us if there is a chance they'll be killed. I won't watch Aidan die. I can't. I can't have any more blood on my hands."

"You won't have to. You'll stop it," Ariana said as she put her hand on Falon's shoulder. "Aidan is your mate, Falon. He is meant to be with you. Besides he's as stubborn as you. I don't believe he will be leaving your side."

Falon shook her head no. "Fate would not be so cruel as to make him stuck with me. Besides, he'll leave as soon as he knows the truth." Falon rubbed the back of her neck.

"Falon, it would not be a punishment to be with you. You're an amazing person. And he won't leave you. Why will you only believe the worst about yourself?"

"No, I'm a screwed up person not an amazing one," Falon said as she looked at her friend skeptically. "He deserves better. And I only believe what is true." She headed back into the cave and found Aidan, Cale, James, Teresa, and the children all waiting patiently. Falon looked at Ariana. "If I can't do this you get them out. Is that understood?"

Ariana nodded, but didn't say anything.

Falon ran her hand through her hair and then looked at the group. "Come on," she said as they headed back into the cave. She looked around and made her way over to Aidan.

"Falon?" Aidan asked as she came over to him, and he saw the look on her face. She looked so defeated, and he didn't like it. He wanted her to be fiery and full of life like she had been since he met her. "What's wrong?" He asked as he brushed her cheek with his fingertips.

"You don't have to go any further, Aidan. I can't promise that it will be safe for you where we are going." Falon spoke as she looked into his green eyes. Everything in her wanted him to stay, but she needed him to be safe, and it just wasn't safe with her.

"I'm not leaving you, and everything is going to be all right," Aidan said as he brushed her cheek with his knuckles. "I promise."

"Very well," Falon said her shoulders drooping even more. "Follow me then," Falon said as she walked away leading the group through a hidden door.

As they entered, they were surrounded by men with weapons. Aidan quickly stepped in front of Falon. He didn't know these men, and he didn't like that they had weapons pointed at his mate.

"Aidan, move. They won't hurt me."

Aidan looked over his shoulder at Falon, "But..,"

"It will be all right," Falon said as she squeezed his hand and walked to the front of the group.

"My Lady," the head guard said as he bowed to her. "Welcome home. We were beginning to wonder if you would return to us."

Aidan and Cale both looked at Falon in shock. Why would a Fae call her Lady?

"Tomas, it's good to see you. As you can see we have brought guest," Falon said giving Tomas an actual smile. "And have I ever not come home?"

"Tomas' lack in faith in you must be failing if he believed you would not return to us," one of the other guards said, as he gave Falon a charming smile.

Finally, the guard turned his attention to the other people in the group. He took in the Fae next to his Lady and noticed that he was looking a tad angry. The guard wondered what that was about, but instead of asking, he turned his attention back towards Falon.

"You are always bringing strays home, My Lady. Come, the council will want to see them. And it is good to have you home again," the Fae said as he bowed to Falon and gave her a wink.

Aidan clenched his fist and jaw, as he saw the look the man was giving *his mate*.

"Very well, Jarus. Lead the way," Falon said as she looked at the guard.

Aidan came up beside her as the guards turned around. "What was all that about?" he snapped out, not happy with the way the other Fae were looking at her. She was his, dammit, and they needed to get that through their heads.

Aidan shook his head to clear out some of the anger. They didn't know she was his mate, so they had no reason not to look at her. That was what the logical part of him was trying to say, but it was not winning against his illogical side. That side was wanting to grab Falon into his arms and scream mine at the top of his lungs. He almost laughed as that picture entered his mind. Yeah, Falon would really enjoy it if he did that. Aidan rolled his eyes as his thoughts continued to go around in circles. He swore he was going insane, and it all started when Falon came into his life.

"I'll explain later." Falon grabbed his hand. "Stay with me, Aidan. And please don't interfere," she said not noticing the way Aidan had snapped.

"I'll only interfere if you are in danger," Aidan said as he laced his fingers in hers. It felt so right to hold her hand. It always felt right. Well, if being with her meant that he lost his sanity then it was totally worth it.

Falon looked down at their hands and for the first time she realized that she had grabbed his hand in hers. "Aidan, I'm sorry," she said so softly that Aidan almost didn't hear her.

"For what?" Aidan asked as he looked down into her face. He didn't understand the pain he was seeing there. He wanted her to smile, to laugh, to get some of her fire back. If this is what coming home did to her, then he was going to get her to leave as soon as possible.

"That you met me. You would have been better off if you had not. You would have been happier, safer." She removed her hand from his and hurried to keep up with the guards.

Aidan looked at her in shock. He hurried to catch up with her, but before he got a chance to talk to her again, they were walking through two large doors. As they entered the room, he saw the two guards who had spoken with Falon hurry ahead and explain that Falon and Ariana had brought some people home with them. Aidan was amazed when he got a look at the twelve men sitting on a platform two feet above them all.

"Bringing home strays again, My Lady," a man said with a laugh.

As Aidan looked around, he noticed that four of the men were Human, four were Fae, and four were Witches. What had they walked into to have all three groups working together?

"Always," Falon said with a small laugh. She then looked behind her and motioned for James and his family to step forward. Falon quickly told them about James and his family, and she wasn't surprised when the Humans stepped up and welcomed them. She nodded towards them giving them the go ahead to leave with a woman. "Annie will take good care of you," Falon said with a small smile. James nodded then left with the woman. Falon turned back to the council and for the first time they noticed Aidan and Cale. "These are..," but before she could finish Jeremiah, the leader of the Fae, was interrupting her.

"Seize them!" Jeremiah called out.

"No!" Falon said, as she and Ariana stepped in front of them. "They are our friends."

"Stand aside, Falon," Jeremiah said his voice deadly.

She cringed at the anger in his voice. He very rarely yelled at her, and he never showed her his anger. Honestly, she had never seen him this way before. It was not like him to lose control over his emotions like this.

"I won't," Falon said standing her ground. Oh, she was so in trouble for this. Several thoughts went through Falon's head at that moment. The main one was, was Aidan worth this? Falon squared her shoulders and waited for a battle because she knew the answer to that. Yes, Aidan was worth this and much, much more.

"Fine, guards remove Falon from this room," Jeremiah said as he spoke to the Fae guards.

Aidan started pulling his powers as the guards came closer. "Anyone of you touch her and you will have to deal with me," Aidan said his voice deadly sounding.

"Aidan, no!" Falon said turning towards him and grabbing his face in her hands. "They will kill you. Let me handle this," she said her voice sounding desperate to even her own ears. "Don't give them a reason to kill you."

Aidan looked down at her and saw the fear in her eyes. No one had the right to make her afraid. "I won't let them hurt you," he said as he grabbed her wrists and brought them away from his face.

"They are not going to hurt me. Please." For once in Falon's life, she let all the walls down and let someone see everything she was feeling. "Please, Aidan. Please."

Aidan sighed and nodded, but he kept his guard up just in case.

"We have never been a people who condemn a man without just cause, and I won't allow it to happen now. Aidan has done nothing wrong," Falon said her voice sounding stronger than she was feeling. This was the first time she had ever stood up to Jeremiah and the other Fae. She saw the shock on everyone's faces, and she knew that things were going to get worse before they got better.

The guards looked at Jeremiah waiting for him to give them the order again, "Guards, take Falon out of this room. Falon, leave this room now!"

"No! I won't allow you to hurt Aidan or Cale," Falon said as she eyed the guards. "I don't wish to hurt anyone, but I cannot allow this. I trained all of you, so I dare you to try."

The guards all looked at her with a look of uncertainty on their faces. They knew that together they probably could take her, but did they really want to risk getting themselves hurt or hurting her? They all looked towards their leader hoping he would somehow tell them what to do.

"You don't understand the situation, Falon. I don't wish to hurt you," Jeremiah said his voice soft as if he was speaking to a child.

"I'm a grown woman. I don't need your protection," Falon said as she crossed her arms in front of her chest.

"Very well," Jeremiah sighed sadly giving Falon a sympathetic look before he turned all his anger to the man standing behind her. "Aidan is the son of Damian," Jeremiah said angrily as he glared at Aidan.

Aidan watched as Falon stiffened at his father's name, and he waited for her to turn and accuse him as everyone else had. He had been paying for his father's sins for years, so why should Falon not treat him as everyone else had?

"Last I checked we did not condemn people based on the actions of their family. If so, then I should have been killed long ago," Falon pinched the bridge of her nose trying to get control of her emotions. She was always dangerous to be around when they were not under control, "Aidan is a good man. He and Cale helped us save James and his family. Plus, they have stepped in and saved our lives more than once. Please, give them a chance."

Aidan looked at Falon in shock. She hadn't accused him or even been angry at him. Instead she had defended him, even after finding out that his father was the worst Fae, no worst being in history. Sometimes Aidan believed he was an even bigger threat than the Elementals who once ruled.

"Do you trust him?" Jeremiah asked as he looked down at Falon. He knew that she did not trust easily. He was hoping that with her denial he would have a way to be rid of Aidan.

Falon looked at Aidan. "Yes, with my life."

Everyone in the room took an intake of breath at what Falon had just said. Everyone in the room knew that Falon did not trust easily, and for her to trust Aidan was a big thing.

Aidan wanted more than anything to grab a hold of her and swing her around. She trusted him. His heart felt like it was going to explode, he was so happy. Trust was the first step for Falon to falling in love with him, and he was bound and determined that she was going to love him.

Jeremiah did not enjoy the way Aidan was looking at Falon. He knew what that look was, and he did not like it. "Fine, we will withhold our judgment for a later time. Falon, since you spoke up, you will be responsible for them both. If they do anything wrong, it will be on your shoulders."

Falon nodded. "I understand."

"I wish to take responsibility for Cale. I brought them here, as well, and Falon should not carry all the blame," Ariana said as she looked towards the Witches. "Father, please allow me to take this on my shoulders as well."

"Ariana, I believe it would be better for you to stay out of this. Let the Fae handle their own kind and us handle ours," Timothy, the head Witch and Ariana's father, said as he looked at his daughter.

"No, Falon was hesitant to bring them here because she was worried about how all of you would react. I was the one who pushed her into

162

this. I should take half of the responsibility," she said not backing down.

Cale leaned over to Aidan. "Why does Falon speak to the Fae and not to the Humans?"

Aidan shrugged his shoulders but kept his eyes on the group. The Fae still looked like they wanted to do harm to him, the Humans looked bored, and the Witches looked only partially curious. Well, all but one. The one on the end looked like he was about to explode he was so angry.

"Very well, but the same goes for you as it does for Falon. They step out of line, and it will be on your head," Timothy said with a small smile. "It has been a while since you have stood your ground on an issue, young one. It is good to see it."

"I understand, and I always stand up for what I believe." She nodded then the four were getting ready to leave when the Witch at the end stood up.

"How can you do this?! If it wasn't for that whore, none of you would have even considered letting him live!" the Witch on the end said with a sneer as he pointed at Falon. "He is Damian's son!"

Jeremiah stood up anger filling him. "You will watch how you speak about my daughter, Jonathan!"

Falon felt a pain shoot through her as she was called a whore, but it wasn't enough of one not to put her hand up to stop Jarus and Tomas from attacking the Witch. They both looked at her with a 'come on look' on their faces, but Falon stood her ground. She did not need a fight to break out between the Witches and Fae all because she was called an ugly name.

Aidan looked at Jeremiah in shock, "Daughter?" he asked in a whisper then he looked down at Falon who had a look on her face that angered him. She looked stunned and hurt. After seeing her expression, the comment the Witch made penetrated his mind. "You need to watch what you say about Falon," he said as he took a step forward.

"Aidan, no," Falon said as he placed her hand on his arm to keep him from going any further. "Stay out of it."

"He called you a..."

Before Aidan could finish, the Witch sent a blast towards him. He was about to block it when Falon yelled, stepped in front of him, and took the blast for him.

"NO!" Falon yelled as she stepped in front of Aidan. As the blast hit her, she felt herself being thrown backwards into Aidan's arms. She felt like all the air inside of her had been knocked out.

"Falon? Falon!" Aidan yelled as he caught Falon in his arms and fell to the ground holding her. "Look at me," he demanded his voice starting to verge on panic sounding as he touched her face and shook her a little. He let out a breath he didn't know he had been holding as she took a breath and began to cough. "That's it, breath," Aidan said as he touched her face gently. Why had she done that? It could have killed her. Aidan held onto her tightly willing her to be all right. "Keep breathing."

Falon felt like her chest was on fire as she tried to breath, but she knew she had to.

"Aidan...," she gasped out trying to warn him that they were still in danger.

Aidan looked up as he felt another surge of energy. As he looked up, he saw another blast coming towards them. He covered Falon and put up a shield, but he had not needed to. As he brought his head up and looked around him, he realized that they were completely surrounded by the Fae.

"You could have killed my daughter!" Jeremiah yelled as he pulled his power.

"She shouldn't have gotten in the way," Jonathan said as he took a step towards the Fae. "That monster deserves to be killed, and so does your daughter if she dares to protect him. I told you years ago that she should be destroyed, and now, she is protecting our enemy! I say kill them both!" he yelled out acting more and more like a mad man.

"No one hurts our Lady," Tomas said as they all began pulling power.

"Yeah," Jarus said agreeing with his commander.

"Enough!" Ariana said as she stepped in between Jonathan and the Fae. "You hurt my friend, Jonathan."

Cale stepped next to Ariana. "This is a bad idea," he said as he powered up to help her.

Aidan looked at Cale and Ariana, and he wondered what was about to happen.

"I can handle this," she said, and with all her power, she threw Jonathan against the wall. The other Witches bowed to her and took a step away from her. They were giving her permission to handle the situation. "You attacked a Fae without permission from the Fae council. Even if I overlooked the fact that you hurt my best friend!" she said in a shout. "I cannot overlook the fact that you disregarded the wishes of the Fae! I won't have a war break out because of your incompetence! The Witch guard will take you to the cells while the council decides what to do with you!" Ariana waved her hand and threw him to the floor where the Witch guard picked him up and dragged him away.

Aidan watched as Cale leaned over and whispered something in Ariana's ear that made her smirk up at him. He then watched as she turned to the council. "I leave his Fate in your hands."

The Fae, Humans, and Witches all nodded towards her. Ariana hurried over to Falon to find that she was still being held by Aidan, and by the paleness of her skin she was not in good shape. "We need to get her to the healers."

Aidan looked back down at Falon and nodded.

"Come on," Ariana said as Aidan scooped Falon up and held her close to his chest.

"Jonas will want to be the one to help her," Jeremiah said as he came over to his daughter. "Follow me. Lady Ariana, you handle things here; I'll go with Falon," he said as he looked at Aidan with an evil look on his face.

Aidan nodded towards Ariana and Cale. He then hurried after Jeremiah. "Falon, keep your eyes open all right," Aidan said softly as he looked down at Falon. As he looked at her he noticed that her eyes were closing, and her breathing was becoming more labored.

Falon looked at Aidan and saw the worry etched into his face. "I'll live."

"Of course you will," Aidan said getting aggravated that she would even think anything else. "I won't let you die," he said his voice strained. Falon went to close her eyes, but Aidan shook her a little. "Keep your eyes on me," he said his voice tense and stubborn sounding.

Falon jerked open her eyes and looked at him, "Stop worrying...you will get wrinkles," she said with a small smile.

Aidan was about to say something when a man with dark, long, brown hair came into the hallway. "What is wrong with Falon?" he asked as he hurried over to her.

"Jonathan hit her with a blast. Of course, it was intended for this guy," Jeremiah said with a sneer at Aidan.

"I didn't ask her to jump in front of it. I would never wish her harm," Aidan said with a snap.

"I don't care what happened. Give me Falon," Jonas said as he reached for her.

"I'll carry her," Aidan said with a growl. There was no way he was letting this pretty boy anywhere near his mate. She was his, and everyone here needed to learn that.

"Give me my sister you son of..."

"Stop, Jonas," Falon said weakly. "Aidan is just trying to protect me."

"Sister?"

"Yes, sister," Jonas said as he tried to remain calm. "Now give me, Falon." Jonas knew that if Falon was defending this Fae, then he couldn't be all bad, but he also knew that his father was not in a good mood right now. Well, he would learn soon enough what was happening.

Aidan looked down at Falon and saw her nod weakly. Reluctantly, he handed her over to Jonas. "I want to stay with her," Aidan said as Jonas turned and went back into the room he had come out of.

"No, you are staying here with me," Jeremiah said as he watched his son and daughter disappear. "You will only be in the way, and Jonas will take care of her. He has been for longer than you have."

Aidan flinched at the anger in the man's voice. "I don't understand what is going on. What is this place?" Aidan asked as he looked at the man next to him.

"Thief's City," Jeremiah said as he rubbed the back of his neck.

Aidan looked at the man in shock, "I thought this place was a myth."

"That is how we like it. Now, we are going to talk about my daughter," Jeremiah said as he eyed Aidan and stressed the *my daughter* part. "I don't know how your paths crossed, but I won't allow my daughter to be with the son of Damian. So whatever ideas you have in your head about her need to leave. Actually, I think it would be better for everyone if you just left."

Aidan felt his chest tightened. Leave Falon. He could never do that. "Falon is a grown woman who can make her own choices. If you think I'm going to back away from you or anyone else, then you are mistaken. Falon is mine," Aidan said through clenched teeth.

"She is my daughter!"

"We both know that is not true. You are a Fae, and she is a Human," Aidan said as he crossed his arms in front of his chest and glared at the man in front of him. He knew he needed to get along with Falon's family, but the idea of someone keeping Falon away from him was making him very angry. "And no one is keeping me away from Falon."

"Listen here, I took her in when she was eight. As far as I'm concerned, she is my daughter," Jeremiah said his voice angry and threatening. "She has been through enough without you playing around with her."

"I'm not playing around with her," Aidan said his anger growing.

"I know your kind," Jeremiah said with a scoff.

"You know nothing about me," Aidan snapped as he got in the Fae's face. "You won't keep me away from her. She is mine, and I keep and protect what is mine," Aidan said with growl as he narrowed his eyes at the man in front of him. Getting along with Falon's family went out the window. No one was keeping her from him.

"If I have to kill you to protect her, I will," Jeremiah said with snap and a coldness that would have made most men back down, but with Aidan, it just made his eyes narrow even more which was a feat considering he looked like he was squinting already.

"Enough!" a voice said from behind them. "You two are acting like children," Jonas said as he looked at the two men. "Father, Falon is very capable of watching out for herself. Which I might add, she does very well. Most of the time," Jonas added under his breath, "And you," Jonas said turning his attention and frustration on Aidan, "you need to learn that Falon is not to be owned. If you wish to stay with her, then you are going to have to win her heart." Jonas then scoffed and added under his breath, "Good luck with that." Jonas then crossed his arms in front of his chest and glared at the two in front of him. "Now, if you two were wondering, Falon is doing fine." Jonas went to walk away when Aidan's voice stopped him.

"May I see her?" Aidan asked his voice sounding tense. He needed to see with his own eyes that Falon was all right. He needed to touch her.

Jonas turned and looked at Aidan. Aidan had tried to cover up his worry in his voice, but Jonas could hear it, and he could see it on his face. "No, she needs her rest, not this," he said waving at Jeremiah and Aidan. "Once she is up and moving, I'm sure she will find you. Now, Father, since I'm her guardian, I believe that you should leave as well. I won't have my sister upset because you are so stubborn. If she does not have a problem being with Aidan, then neither should you." With that, Jonas turned around and walked back into the room. Aidan looked at the door and frowned. He then put his back to the wall and slid down it until he was sitting on the floor.

"What are you doing?" Jeremiah asked his voice sounding as tired as he felt. He could try to protect Falon, but he knew that ultimately it was up to her, and she did have a way of not wanting to be protected.

"I'm staying here," Aidan said as he looked up at Falon's father.

"Very well, but don't expect Jonas to be nice about you sitting out here," with that Jeremiah left.

"I won't leave her," Aidan said as he put his head against the wall. This day had not gone the way he had planned. For some reason, he had imagined them coming to Falon's home, him telling her how he felt, and everything being all right after that. He had never imagined this. Aidan closed his eyes and tried to let the stress go, but instead, all he kept seeing was her getting hurt and falling into his arms not breathing. He swore she took a good hundred years off of his life. Aidan sighed deeply as he thought about how his life had changed since meeting Falon. It was true that his job had been dangerous, but now, it seemed like he didn't get a moments peace. Of course, he also got the joy of being with Falon all the time which definitely made up for all the problems. She was worth every trouble that had and would come his way. He knew that together they would be just fine, but if he lost her, he knew deep in his soul that he would also lose his reason for living. In just a short time, she had become his everything, and he knew that with time that feeling would only deepen and grow. As Aidan continued to think about Falon, he heard someone clearing their throat beside him.

Aidan opened his eyes to see Jonas staring down at him, "She will be fine. No need to frown in that manner. Now, come."

"I thought you said..."

"I know what I said, but Falon was not in the mood to speak with our father. We love him, but he can be a tad over bearing at times. Especially, if he gets an idea in his head, and right now, he has the idea that you are going to hurt Falon. And since Falon tends to be just as stubborn, they would have ended up fighting, and she was not up to that."

"I would not hurt her. I..."

Jonas put up his hand to stop him. "Falon has pleaded your case to me, but that does not mean I trust you. She is very important to me and all the Fae here. But as you said, she is a grown woman." Jonas put out his hand and helped Aidan up, "If you hurt her in any way, I'll kill you and not feel bad about it at all."

Aidan nodded his head in understanding. "I won't hurt her."

Jonas looked at the man in front of him and for some reason he believed him. "Very well," Jonas turned around and led Aidan inside the room.

Aidan felt his heart stop as he came in and saw Falon laying on a bed with her eyes closed. If it had not been for the rise and fall of her chest, he would have believed she was dead; she was so white. "She will be fine, right?"

"Stop worrying," Falon said as she opened her eyes and looked at Aidan. "I have had worse than this. Tell him, Bubby."

Jonas chuckled. "Yes our little adventurer has had quite a few bumps and bruises along the way. Most happening in the last year," Jonas said eying her suspiciously. "It is almost as if you are taking more chances." The playfulness was gone from his voice and Aidan could see he was serious.

"I take no more chances than normal," Falon said as she picked at her finger nails.

"You, my little sister, need to work on becoming a better liar." He then kissed her on the forehead, "I'll leave you two alone." Jonas then walked out of the room.

Aidan came over to Falon and brushed her cheek with his thumb, "Why?"

Falon tilted her head and looked at him in confusion. "Why what, Aidan?" She loved it when he touched her. It made her feel safe. Like nothing bad could ever happen to her. Which was silly, considering she had just almost been killed by a blast from a Witch. Actually, if she had been a normal Human, she would have been killed.

"Why did you step in front of me? You could have been killed," Aidan said as he cupped the sides of her face. He needed her to realize what could have happened. He needed her to realize that he needed her to be all right.

"It was reaction," Falon said with a shrug. "Jonas, fixed me up, so I'm fine. There is no need to worry," she said with a small smile. Why was Aidan making such a big deal about this? Falon was confused about his reaction. Could he care for her?

"No need to worry?" Aidan asked his voice growing louder. "You could have been killed! What then?"

"I would be dead, so it would not concern me," Falon said with a tone that said she was not going to discuss this further. "Now, I do believe that I need to show you to your room," she said as she sat completely up and swung her feet over the edge of the bed.

"No, you will rest. I'll stay here with you," Aidan said his voice growing panicky as she went to stand up. "Lay back down, now!" Aidan yelled as he looked at her with a stern look on his face.

Falon looked at him in shock. "Fine, man you are not in a good mood," she said as she laid back down. If she had been stronger, she would have fought him more, but she really did not have the energy for a fight with Aidan.

Aidan looked down at her, his heart slowing down as she laid back down. "We are going to come to an understanding, you and I."

"Are we now?" Falon asked as she closed her eyes a small smile playing at the corner of her mouth. He was dreaming if he thought she was going to agree to anything.

"Yes," Aidan said as he started to pace. "You're going to start taking fewer chances, or I'm going to have a...," before Aidan could finish, he realized that Falon had fallen fast asleep. "What am I going to do with you?" he asked sweetly as he kissed her on the forehead.

"Take care of her and watch her back," Jonas said softly as he came into the room. Aidan cleared his throat not liking that someone saw him acting so soft. "Don't worry, I won't tell anyone that you are not as mean as you act," Jonas chuckled at Aidan's face.

"I plan on taking care of her. I don't wish to see her die," Aidan said as he turned to look at Jonas.

"Well, you have your work cut out for you. Falon has always taken chances, but this past year her chances have become more like suicide attempts." Jonas rubbed the back of his neck, "When she said that she has had worse than this, she was not kidding. I swear she has taken off several hundred years of my life."

"Why is she doing it? From what I have learned about her, she is stubborn but not suicidal," Aidan said quietly as he looked back at Falon. He didn't want her waking up before he got more information from her brother. If Jonas was willing to talk to him, then he was going to let him talk. He wanted to know everything he could about Falon.

"She has lived through a lot, and she does not allow anyone in to help her with the pain. I believe that it is getting to her, and she does not know how to deal with it. Of course, instead of getting help from one of us, she just takes more risks to try and push the nightmares away." Jonas put his hand on Aidan's shoulder. "My sister means a lot to me, but she won't let me help her, and I'm the closest one to her."

"What about Ariana?"

"They are close, but Falon won't tell her about her past. Ariana knows some, but not everything." Jonas shrugged, "When we found Falon she was eight years old, but she had been living on her own since she was five. For three years, she lived alone and that is not even the worst of it."

"Why are you telling me this?" Aidan asked as he brushed Falon's hand with his own. He needed to touch her, and he did not know why.

Jonas watched the gently gesture and smiled. "Because you're her mate."

Aidan's eyes widened, "I...we are not..." he couldn't even finish because of the look Jonas was giving him. "I haven't told her," he said as he looked at Jonas his shoulders sagging. "I don't think she'll take it well."

Jonas laughed, "Probably not, but it would not be because she did not like you. Actually, by the way she protected you and the way she spoke to me about you, I would say that she is on her way to falling in love with you, if she is not all ready there."

"Then why would she not handle it well?" Aidan asked his voice a little lighter than before. He hoped she was in love with him. He needed her to be in love with him.

"Her life is...," Jonas stopped trying to pick the best word, "complicated, and she won't want you to be drawn into it. She is a protector to everyone she cares about. Even if that means giving up something or in this case, someone she cares about. She would rather be unhappy than to see you die," Jonas said as he ran his hand through his hair, "More than likely, knowing her, she will try to push you away."

"She can get over that. If anyone needs a protector, it's her. And I'm not going anywhere," Aidan said as he laced his fingers with hers. She was his mate, and he was just going to have to get her to open up to him. She had said that she trusted him with her life, but would she trust him with her heart?

"Good. Just remember that when she is giving you fits because she will. She will use whatever means necessary to get you to leave her. It is what she does. Only when she knows that you won't leave will she stop," Jonas patted Aidan on the back, kissed Falon on the forehead, and left the room. Leaving Aidan alone with Falon and his thoughts.

Chapter Nine

"He is driving me insane," Falon said as she leaned against the wall and looked at Ariana.

"I think he isn't and that's what is bothering you. I believe that you have been enjoying his company these last two days," Ariana said with a knowing smile.

Falon sighed as she pushed off the wall and walked over to the window. "I need to stay away from him."

"Why?"

"Because I...I'm...," Falon shook her head, but before she could finish, Aidan walked into the room. "Seriously!"

"Where have you been?" Aidan asked as he came over to Falon. He had been looking everywhere for her. He didn't know why, but for some reason, when he didn't know where she was his chest tightened, and he felt like he was having trouble breathing. It was probably because of her getting hurt so badly when they first got here. Aidan rubbed the back of his neck and hoped that it would slack up soon. He would like to go a few minutes without feeling like he was having a panic attack, because he couldn't find her. Of course, if she would cooperate and let him know where she was going, then it wouldn't be a problem, but no, she had to try and avoid him. It was really getting annoying. They had been in this bloody city for two days, and in those two days, he hadn't even been able to kiss her once.

"What are you, my mother? Man, you need to back off some," Falon said as she headed out of the room. When Aidan went to follow, she turned on him with a very upset look on her face. "No, you stay," she said pointing to the room. "I go. You stay," she said her voice slow as she talked to him. She then turned on her heels and walked away.

"Hey!" Aidan yelled after her, "I'm not some pet that you can tell to stay!" He yelled as he caught up with her and grabbed her arm to get her to look at him.

"Then why are you following me around?!" she asked as she looked into his beautiful green eyes. Man, she shouldn't have done that if she had wanted to act angry at him. This man was driving her insane, and it wasn't because he was following her around. In the past two days, she had tried to do everything she could think of to get him to hate her, but still, he followed her. She needed to get him to hate her. It was the only way to keep him safe. Didn't he realize how much trouble she was? He should considering they had almost been killed too many times already.

Falon sighed knowing that if he stayed around, it would only be a matter of time before he was killed. She shook her head knowing that she couldn't let that happen. No, she wouldn't let that happen. She cared too much for him to watch him die. She had thought she could make memories with him, but now, she knew she couldn't. She couldn't risk something happening to him before he left. She would not watch him die or leave.

"No matter what you do, no matter what you say, I'm not going anywhere," Aidan said his voice tense and strong. He was not letting her go. He couldn't. She was a part of him now, and nothing was going to change that.

"Aidan..," Falon's voice broke and that irritated her, "please."

"No," with that, Aidan brought his lips down to hers. As she wrapped her arms around his neck, he pushed her against the wall, deepening the kiss. When he pulled back they were both breathless, "I'll never let you go. You, Falon, are my mate. You are mine." He had finally told her. She would either accept it or she wouldn't, but he had told her.

Falon dropped her head and shook her head no, "Fate would not be that cruel to you." She then pushed away from him, "Aidan, you deserve better." She then ran off. She needed to get away from him. She needed to get her head on straight. When he was around, all she could do was think about him and how he made her feel. It wasn't right to do this to him. He deserved better than her. He deserved someone sweet and kind and...and pure. Falon covered her face with her hands and headed to her room. She needed to think.

Aidan was shocked by her words and by the tears he had seen in her eyes. She was usually so strong and stubborn, but as he had looked into her eyes, it had been as if she was broken. Aidan shook his head before he started after her, but as he went to go after her, he was stopped by Ariana. "Give her time, Aidan."

"I don't understand her," Aidan said as he ran his hand through his hair. "I know she cares for me, but..."

"I know. Let me go talk to her," Ariana said then she left Aidan alone and went after her friend. When she came into Falon's room, she saw something that she never thought she would see. She found Falon crying on her bed. "Falon," Ariana said softly as she sat down on the bed and ran her hand down Falon's dark, red hair.

"I can't do this. It isn't fair to him," Falon said between sobs. "Fae pride themselves in their mates, and I'm nothing to be proud of. I'm not even an innocent anymore," Falon said as her voice filled with shame as she turned away from Ariana.

"That was not your fault, and he would be proud to have you. You are an amazing person."

"He would not be proud if he knew the truth. He would not be if he knew what a monster I am," Falon said as she sat up and brought her knees to her chest. "Ariana, I can't stay here and do this to myself. I can't do this to him. I have to leave," she said as she put her head on her knees. For the first time in her life, she truly felt defeated. For the first time, she felt like dying. She had always played with death to get the shadows of her past to leave, but now, she wanted to welcome it. Anything to forget who and what she was. Anything to save her from the look of disgust and horror that would be on Aidan's face when he found out the truth. She knew she wouldn't survive his hatred or him leaving her. Falon didn't know how, but in the short time that they had been together, he had come to mean a great deal to her.

"No, you just need time. Why don't you just talk to him?" Ariana said her voice shaking with emotion. If Falon left, she was going with her, with or without Cale. She could not let her friend go off on her own like this. "Why do you not rest and in the morning we will talk about this some more."

Falon nodded her head then laid down her back facing Ariana. She closed her eyes waiting for Ariana to leave. Falon knew what she had to do. Maybe, Fate would cooperate this time. Maybe, this time Fate would be on her side.

~~~

Aidan stopped pacing as soon as he saw Ariana come out of Falon's room. The hope he had in him when she said she would talk to Falon died when he saw the sadness in Ariana's eyes. "She would not talk to you?"

Ariana sat down on the couch and put her head in her hands, "I have never seen her like this before. She has always been so full of fire. Even at her darkest times, she was a fighter. Right now, it's as if she has decided to stop. To stop fighting and living. I don't understand it."

"I'm doing this to her." Aidan said as he continued pacing, "I won't have her like this. If I leave will she go back to the way she was?" Aidan asked as he rubbed the back of his neck. The mere thought of leaving her was making him feel sick, but if it helped her then he would do it. Aidan knew he could not stand by and watch her slowly fall apart. He just couldn't.

"It would not do any good," Ariana said as she looked up with tears in her eyes, "It is as if she has broken, and I don't know how to fix it. Falon has always been the strong one, but she has also always held in her troubles. I think they have finally all hit her, and she is having trouble dealing with them."

Cale came out of his room and saw how upset Ariana was. He hurried over to her and wrapped his arms around her. Aidan watched the embrace and his heart broke. He wanted to be able to comfort Falon like that, but she wouldn't let him. Aidan swore under his breath and left the room. He needed to get his head on straight. He needed to figure out a way to get through to Falon. As he hurried through the corridors, he ran into Jonas. "Aidan, what has you so upset, my friend?"

Aidan looked at Jonas, the man who had become his friend in only two days. It was odd considering Aidan had never been good with people, but no matter what he said, Jonas took it all in stride. "Falon, she...I don't know what I can do to fix it."

Jonas sighed sadly. "Come walk with me," he said as he turned and walked back towards the rooms Aidan had come from, "You coming into her life has made her have to face her demons. Before, she could ignore them, but now she can't. She's strong; she'll recover."

"I know she's strong, but you didn't see her face earlier. All the fire that I have grown to love was gone, and in its place was an emptiness I didn't like," Aidan said with a sadness to his voice that wasn't like him. He normally hid his emotions, but he knew that with Jonas it was pointless. Somehow Jonas could see right through him.

Jonas looked at Aidan, "She is afraid that if you know the truth you won't want her. That you will leave her."

"I won't leave her," Aidan said his voice filled with aggravation. "I love her!" He froze when those words came out of his mouth. He had known he was coming to love her, but he hadn't thought he was there yet. Had he already fallen in love with her? As he thought about it, he knew it was true. He loved her. Man, that had happened faster than he thought was possible.

Jonas smiled at him, "I know."

"Then help me," Aidan said as he grabbed Jonas by the shoulders.

"It is going to take more than words to get her to see that you love her," Jonas said as they went back to walking and came to the door that led them to Ariana and Falon's living area.

"What am I going to have to do to prove it?" Aidan asked as him and Jonas stood at the door.

"Stay and be constant. She has very few people in her life who are constant," Jonas patted him on the back then walked into the room. When they came in Jonas chuckled. "You two need to cool it before the Witches find out," he said as they came in and caught Cale and Ariana making out.

Aidan shook his head still amazed that Cale's mate was a Witch. Of course, he was even more amazed that his mate was a Human being raised as a Fae. No wonder Falon had difficulties with who she was. She was a Human living in a Fae world and using Witch power. Anyone would be confused. He shook his head, but soon he was smiling as Jonas' words penetrated his mind. Jonas was right, if the Witches caught Cale and Ariana making out that much, there would be some kind of ceremony shortly after. Aidan smirked as he wondered if it would be a bonding ceremony or a burial ceremony.

Ariana pulled back her face turning red, while Cale leaned back against the couch and pulled her tightly to him looking rather smug at the moment. "Are you here to talk to Falon?" Ariana asked trying to get the focus off of her and Cale.

"Yes, is she in her room?" Jonas asked with a smile. It was good to see Ariana happy. He hoped Falon would follow her lead and become happy as well. Jonas' smile faded as he went to the door. Falon had always been so open with him, but lately, she had closed off more. He told everyone she would be fine, but he wondered if that was true. "Aidan, stay here. Let me have a moment alone with her."

Aidan nodded then he watched as Jonas opened the door

"Dammit!" Jonas' voice rang out from the room.

Panic filled Aidan as he heard the hurt and anger in Jonas' voice. As he came into the room, he saw why Jonas was so upset. Falon's room was empty, and her window was open.

"Be safe, little sis," Jonas said as he looked out the window.

"Where is she?" Aidan asked dreading the answer. *Please don't tell me what I think you're going to tell me*, he pleaded in his mind as he looked at Jonas.

"Gone," Jonas said as he turned from the window and went to walk out of the room.

"Gone where?" Aidan asked as he grabbed Jonas by the arm and stopped him.

"I don't know, but I promise you I'll find her," Jonas said as he looked at Aidan with a look of hurt and determination on his face. He couldn't believe that Falon had done something so stupid. If it was the last thing he did, he was going to knock some sense into his little sister.

Aidan hurried over to the window and looked down. "How did she get out?" The thought of her climbing out the window made his stomach tighten and his heart speed up. It wasn't an impossible climb, but it would have been very difficult. Aidan looked at the ground just to make sure she wasn't laying there bleeding and broken. He let out a sigh of relief as he saw that the ground was empty of her body. However, the relief was soon replaced by pure anger and fear as he realized that Falon had left him, and she was all alone. What if something happened to her before he could get to her?

"She's a good climber," Jonas said sarcastically. "Aidan, I'll be able to find her. Just give me time," he said as he rubbed the back of his neck.

"Time? Time! Falon is a magnet for trouble. I have to find her now!" Aidan yelled as he went to leave the room.

"Aidan wait," Jonas said as he followed Aidan out into the sitting area. "I know how to track her. I know how she hides. You don't. You'll never be able to find her," Jonas yelled before Aidan could open the door to leave the living area completely. He needed Aidan to understand that if Falon did not wish to be found then he would be the only one who could find her. Jonas also knew that if anyone was capable of knocking some sense into her it would be him, not Aidan. Aidan would probably just make the matter worse and not even realize it.

Aidan paused at the door. "I have to find her. I can't lose her," he said his voice filled with more emotion than he even knew he was capable of.

"What is going on?" Ariana asked with a panic overtaking her voice.

"Falon is gone," Jonas said softly.

"But...she...," Ariana slowly sat down on the couch, "she left without me?" she ask as tears filled her eyes, "Jonas, if she left without me then she doesn't plan to..."

"I know," Jonas said as he looked at Ariana with a sadness in his eyes that was unlike him.

"She doesn't plan to what?!" Aidan asked in a yell. What the hell were they talking about? "What doesn't she plan to do?!"

"It does not matter. I'll bring her home," Jonas said with a determined look on his face.

Cale looked at the sadness on Ariana's face then he looked at Aidan who looked so lost. "We're good trackers. We can find her," he said more to Aidan than anyone else. He knew that if it was Ariana missing he would be beside himself with panic and worry.

Ariana shook her head. "No, Jonas is right. He is the only one who'll be able to find her. You don't know Falon like he does. She will hide, and we would never be able to find her."

"How can you find her?" Aidan asked turning towards Jonas. What made Jonas so special that he was the only one who could fine Falon? Aidan ran his hand through his hair in frustration. He should be the one going after Falon. She was his mate.

"When I became her guardian, I connected with her. I'll be able to use that connection to get an idea of where she is. After I do that, I'll be able to find her location based on how she thinks." Jonas walked over to Aidan and put his hands on the man's shoulders. "I'll find her."

With that, Jonas left the room and disappeared. Cale went over to talk to Aidan, but Aidan shrugged him off and went into Falon's room, shutting the door behind him. Once in the room, Aidan walked over to the window. "Come back to me," he begged as he fell to his knees. The pain of her leaving hitting him full force.

Chapter Ten

Falon was drunk, dead drunk. She had never been a drinker before, but a couple of hours ago it had sounded like a good idea. For the past three weeks, she had tried to forget everything and everyone, especially, Aidan. *It was better this way,* she thought grimly as she took another swig of the bottle she was carrying in her hand. She thought about the last three weeks and cringed. She had run into one fight after another, and yet, she was still alive. If she hadn't been trying to get herself killed then she would have been killed. Wasn't Fate a fickle thing. When she was trying to stay alive, she almost died, and when she wanted to die, she couldn't. Fate sucked. As she continued to walk, or rather stumble, down the street she came face to face with three or was it six Witches. Falon squinted her eyes trying to get them to stop moving.

"Move out of the way you, idiots," Falon slurred. Hey, maybe this was her lucky day. Maybe, Fate was back to working right.

"Well, you have either gotten braver or dumber, Falon," one of the Witches sneered.

"I...would...go...with dumber, Amos," Falon said as she swayed on her feet. "Now, will you six stop moving so I can kill you," she said her vision blurring and wavering making the three Witches turn into six moving ones again. Man, she wished they would stop moving. It was starting to make her really sick.

"She's drunk. This should be easy," one of the others said with a laugh.

"Knowing my luck lately," Falon said then stopped and closed her eyes to keep herself from throwing up, "probably not."

As Falon faced off with the Witches, she waited for them to send a blast her way, but before they could, a masked figure appeared behind them.

"I want this one," the figure said with a growl.

Falon watched as the figure took care of the three/six Witches with little problem then advanced on her. Great, Fate was really getting on her nerves. Falon thought about stopping this figure just on the principle alone, but she didn't. She didn't fight as the figure neared. She just stood there. As he got closer, she backed herself up until her back was pressed against the stone wall that surrounded the town she was outside of. It was the town she had met Aidan in. A pain shot through her as her mind went to Aidan. She wondered if he had even noticed she was missing. A part of her told her yes, he would have noticed and that he would be worried, but the other part told her that he wouldn't notice or care.

Falon shook her head and tried to focus on the figure coming closer to her. She wasn't shocked when the figure grabbed her roughly and slammed her against the wall. She didn't even flinch or cringe when he put a knife to her throat. Yeah, she was really proud of that, and the fact that she hadn't even tried to fight. This time her instincts and Fate were going to lose. This guy would definitely get the job done.

"Is this what you want?!" the figured yelled out at her. "Do you want me to kill you?"

Falon squinted at him and wondered why his voice sounded so familiar. She knew that in the deep part of her mind she knew that voice, but as drunk as she was, she just could not recognize it. "Yes. This is what I want," she said softly as a tear slide down her face. This was what she wanted. She wanted the pain and memories to end. She wanted to die. Falon closed her eyes waiting for death, but in the end, Fate laughed at her once more. It would seem that only Fate would choose how and when she died. She cursed Fate as the masked figure loosened his grip on her and the knife fell to the ground.

"Is your life so bad?" he asked softly.

Falon looked at the figure, and without any thought, she moved her hand to his mask and took it off. Maybe, if she revealed his identity he would reconsider. Maybe she could still beat Fate. "Jonas?" she asked as she stared into his face. Crap, Fate won this round. Again.

"Answer the question, Falon!" Jonas said coldly. He couldn't believe that his little sister had fallen this hard. Jonas shook his head as he took in the bruises on her face, her drunken manner, and the dark circles under her eyes. She was really a mess. He sighed sadly as he realized that Falon was truly broken, and she hadn't come to him. She hadn't asked for help. Instead, she had searched out some way to end her life without doing it by her own hand.

"I can't live like this anymore," Falon said as she slide down the wall and put her head in her hands. "Please, Jonas, do this for me," Falon pleaded as she looked up into his eyes. "Please!"

Jonas felt his heart break as tears streamed down Falon's face.

"Do it!" she screamed out at him making him flinch. "I took away your mate. I ruined your chances at a family!" Falon screamed. She then covered her ears as another set of memories hit her. "I can't live like this. I destroy everything I touch. I'll destroy, Aidan. I'll destroy my family." Falon could not control the sobs that overtook her. She put her head in her hands and let the tears fall.

Jonas knelt in front of his sister and pulled her into his arms. "Claudia wasn't your fault. She made her own choice," Jonas said as he kissed her hair and rocked her gently. He remembered a time when Falon was a little girl, and some of the other children had been making fun of her. She had come to him and crawled up in his lap. Back then, she had thought that he could solve all her problems with a gentle voice and a kiss. Now, she wanted him to end her life. Jonas closed his eyes and put his cheek to the top of her head. "You won't destroy Aidan or any of us. You're a good person. You would rather die than hurt someone you care about. I wish you could see what we all see. I wish you could see what I see. I see a wonderful, beautiful, sweet person who is full of fire and love. I see a fierce protector and friend. Please Falon, please, come home. You are my world, Little Sister," Jonas begged his voice breaking. "I can't lose you. I know you have been through a lot, and I'm sorry. I wish I could take it all away. I wish that it could be like it was when you were little. I wish I could just tell you it would be all right, and you would believe me like you use to." Jonas held Falon close as she cried.

"Aidan will never understand. He won't want me anymore. I can't....I can't watch him leave me," Falon said as she buried her head into her brother's chest like she used to when she was a little girl. Jonas always could make everything better. He always understood her better than anyone else.

"You underestimate how much he loves you," Jonas said as he rocked her in his arms.

"He doesn't love me. He doesn't even know me," Falon said slowly.

"Oh, but he does, and you love him."

"He deserves..."

Jonas pulled back and grabbed her face in between his hands. "He deserves to be with you. The woman he loves. Come home. Please, Falon," Jonas begged, his eyes pleading to her from the depths of his soul.

Falon looked at him and saw the sadness she was causing. She sighed deeply and hung her head. Now that Jonas had found her, he would not let her go. He would just follow her until she changed her mind, or until he died trying to protect her from herself. "I'll go back. I'm also going to tell him everything. Once he leaves then you have to promise to let me go," she said as she looked up into Jonas' eyes hoping for understanding.

"He won't leave you," Jonas said with a small smile avoiding making any such promise. He would always come after her.

Falon looked at him skeptically, but she didn't say anything else. She just buried her head against his chest and fell asleep.

Jonas sighed deeply, scooped Falon up into his arms, and carried her to a safe place to sleep off the worse of the alcohol. He would get her back home, then the rest was up to Aidan.

Chapter Eleven

Aidan gazed out the window in Falon's room. It had been four weeks, four torturous weeks, since Falon had disappeared. Cale and Ariana were now joined; he was happy for them, but he was also angry. He should be holding Falon in his arms right now, not wondering if she was even alive. He closed his eyes and pictured her face. Somehow he knew that she was still alive, but that didn't ease up the tension or worry. He should have gone with Jonas or at least followed him. Well, he had tried following, but Jeremiah and Cale along with a few others had stopped him and told him that he would only be in the way. After the fifth time of trying to go after Falon, he had given up and permanently camped out in Falon's room. He loved this room. It made him feel closer to her, connected somehow. It also gave him insight into who Falon really was.

Falon came into the room to see Aidan staring out the window. Her heart lifted at the sight of him. Why was it that just being near him made her feel whole? It was as if after all these years of not feeling like she had ever truly found a home, she now had one, but it was Aidan, not an actual place. Falon sighed then finally quietly spoke, "Aidan?"

Aidan turned around as someone called his name. "Falon? Falon!" he yelled as he hurried over to her, picked her up, and swung her around. He had just placed her on the ground when she looked up at him. She looked horrible. She was pale, had lost weight, had dark circles under her eyes, and she looked like she had been in a fight. Aidan cupped her face with his hands and rubbed her cheeks with his thumbs. "Don't do that to me again. I have been worried sick about you. I thought I'd never see you again," he said sternly. He was about to say something else when she pulled out of his hold. Aidan wanted desperately to pull her back into his arms. All he wanted to do was hold her, but every time he made a move for her she would draw back more.

"I...I need to tell you something," Falon said not meeting his gaze. "I need you to listen and not interrupt. Once I've finished, if you want to leave, I'll understand," she said her voice filled with all the sadness and heartache she had felt over the years. Jonas knew a lot about her past, but she had never spoken to him about it. Aidan would be the first person she had ever spoken to about it.

Aidan grabbed her gently by the arms. "I'm not leaving you. What will it take for you to understand that?! You are my mate! I'm meant to be with you!" Aidan yelled, shaking her a little as he did.

Falon shrugged out of his grip. "Sit," she said motioning for a chair. Her voice was emotionless.

Aidan sighed sadly and sat down.

"The first thing I'm going to tell you is not in order. Once I tell you this, I'll tell you everything in order." Falon focused her attention firmly on Aidan. "Just because I'm your mate does not mean you have to be with me." Falon put up her hand when he went to speak. "Hear me then you may talk. Jonas had a mate. Her name was Claudia, and he met her fifteen years ago. One night, while I was sleeping, she slipped into my room and tried to slit my throat."

Aidan took in a sharp breath. He watched as she shrugged then continued on with the story as if it wasn't her past they were discussing but someone else's.

"Lucky for me Jonas followed her. According to him, she had been acting suspiciously, and it caused him to be concerned." Falon closed her eyes and sighed sadly her shoulders sagging under the memory. "He ended up killing her to save me." Her voice broke and Aidan wanted so bad to hold her, but as he reached for her, she moved out his reach. "That is not even the worse thing I have done." She rubbed her arms with her hands trying to rid herself of the cold chill that always accompanied her memories.

"You did not do that," Aidan said standing up and facing Falon. How could she think that was her fault? It wasn't her fault that Jonas' mate had tried to kill her. I mean, she couldn't have been any older than ten. She had just been a baby.

"Let me finish. Please," Falon said pleadingly.

Aidan sat back down and nodded for her to continue.

"Now, I'm going to tell you some things and you may want to interrupt," she said giving him a raised eyebrow, "but please don't or we will never get this over with."

"I promise to keep my mouth shut until you finish," Aidan said giving her a charming smile.

Falon gave him a ghost of a smile as she ran her hand through her hair, "All right. Now, first thing you need to know is that I was raised at first by a Witch." Falon played with her Witches stone. "He was one of the oldest ones still alive at the time. He had taken me from my father to protect me from the Elementals." Aidan looked at her with a confused expression on his face, but he did not say anything. "My mother and father were not the same. My mom was a Human." Falon sat down in a chair and put her hand under her chin. "My father was a...," Falon stopped and looked away from Aidan, "Elemental."

Aidan took in a sharp intake of breath. What? That could not be possible. All the Elementals had been destroyed a thousand years ago. He should know; he helped kill them all. A thousand questions ran through his head as he listened to Falon. How could this even be possible?

Falon avoided looking at Aidan because she didn't want to see fear and anger in his eyes. "My mother was just a regular woman who my father used. It had been the first time that any child had been born without both parents being Elementals." Falon shook her head. "I guess that's why the Witch thought he could raise me differently. The Witch watched and waited and before my father could claim me from my mother, the Witch stole me. He protected me. As the war raged on, he knew that it would be only a matter of time before both sides found out about me. So when I was five, he put a Witch's stone around my neck, put a letter in my pocket, and used all of his power to hide me from everyone. At least, that's what I remember."

"How?" Aidan asked, he closed his eyes in frustration when he remembered he was not supposed to ask anything.

Falon pressed on. "I don't know. All I know is that I woke up in an alley not knowing where I was or even what time I was in. I lived on the streets for three years before I found out that I had..." Falon stopped for a minute trying to find the right word, "I guess you could say disappeared for a thousand years. Talk about confusing." Falon stood up and went over to the window.

Aidan looked at her in shock. He bet it was confusing. Being in one time then waking up in another would be hard on anyone, especially a child. He had lived during that time, and he knew a lot had changed. Plus, she had just been a baby. She should have been being protected, not left alone to fend for herself.

"It was awhile later before I finally found a home." By this time, Falon had unlaced the leather band on her wrist, and she was tracing the brand on her arm. It was a brand that all Elementals were born with, just like all Fae had a tattoo on their necks and all Witches had gold or silver eyes. It was the way they were distinguished from the other groups. "I was hungry, so I tried to pickpocket Jeremiah. He thought it was extremely entertaining. He took me home with him. It was not until three

214

months later that he saw the tattoo." Falon shrugged. "By then I had already become a part of the Fae family, and I had become best friends with the Witch leader's daughter, Ariana. So after finding out what I was, Jeremiah and Timothy got together and decided to protect me. Jeremiah because he was already starting to think of me as his daughter and because Jonas had taken such a liken to me. Timothy, because I had become friends with Ariana. Actually, I was Ariana's only friend. Anyway, after that the Fae protected me. At least most of them. I have had some...difficulties over the years," Falon said as she searched for the right word to describe what she'd been through. "Even though only a select few knew about me, some others still found out. Ever since some of these incidents, I have become even more closed up, more secretive. Most of the time, I don't even use my powers. I stick to the Witches stone or my own physical strength. To be honest, I hate my powers, and I would rather not use them at all. Sometimes I have no choice, but if it is possible, I find another way to deal with the situation." Falon ran her hand through her hair, and she was so frustrated that it shook. "Anyway that's not important right now."

It was taking everything in Aidan not to grab Falon and hold her, to tell her that she didn't have to tell him anymore if she didn't want to. He wanted her to. He wanted to know everything, but as he watched her hand shake and her face twist in pain, he didn't know if he could put her through this. "Falon.."

"No, I need to tell you the rest. I lived in moderate peace until I was fifteen. I mean there were those who would find out what I was and try to slit my throat like Claudia, but for the most part, it was peaceful." Falon shrugged.

Aidan was impressed how she just brushed it all off, but it also bothered him. If those incidents were nothing to her what else had she been through?

"At fifteen, I came into my powers, and they scared me. By this time, I had learned all about the Elementals, and I didn't want to turn out like them. My powers were strong and scary, so I left. I was afraid that I'd hurt someone on accident. My powers always seemed to have a mind of their own. I constantly was putting out fires. Jonas called me his little fire bug for a while. He thought it would make me laugh, but all it did was worry me more. I was terrified I would become like the others, or that I would hurt someone I loved. Especially, him and Ariana considering they were the ones I was around all the time."

Aidan couldn't imagine what it had been like for her. He knew that Elemental children were raised around the power so they would not fear it, but she had not been. She had been taught the complete opposite. To fear her powers. On top of all that, Falon was the fire Elemental, the most powerful of all the other Elementals. Her powers would have been hard to control.

Aidan shook his head wondering how she had managed it and not given in to the pull of its power. How had she managed to put it to the side and not use it very often? Aidan ran his hand through his hair knowing what he was going to have to do. He was going to have to get her to use her power, or one day, it was going to explode inside of her. She needed to learn to control it and use it without fear of something bad happening. Only then would she become the woman she was meant to be. Aidan almost laughed when he thought about her eyes turning red when she was angry; he knew now why he thought that color had suited her. It was because her eyes were meant to be red.

"I didn't tell anyone where I was going. It was a stupid thing to do," Falon said as she wrapped her arms around her waist.

Her comment pulled Aidan out of his thoughts and had him wondering what she was going to say next.

"I was captured by Amos and handed over to Damian and his men."

Falon's voice had taken on a tense and strained tone that Aidan had never heard. The mention of his father had Aidan's mind imagining all the horrible things that could happen to a fifteen year old girl at the hands of his father. Fear crept into his heart as he saw the pain in her eyes. What had his father done to her? Aidan knew that his father was pure evil. He knew what his father was capable of. It was the reason why Aidan had not spoken to him in a thousand years. It was the reason that Aidan and Cale fought against him. He couldn't imagine what Falon had gone through.

"I was held captive for a year before Jonas and the others could rescue me. After that, Jonas connected himself with me so that he would be able to find me." Falon went over to the window and held onto the ledge. "I lost my innocence in there. I lost a part of me. The things they did to me...." Falon shook her head as tears escaped her eyes. She hadn't meant to say that last part, but she couldn't help it. It had just come out.

Aidan felt anger enter him as he heard the pain in her voice. If it was the last thing he did, he was going to kill his father for what he had done to her. No one touched his Falon, and no one hurt her. "Falon, I'm so sorry," he said his voice breaking with emotion. He stood up and came over to her.

Falon tensed as Aidan turned her to face him, but she relaxed into him when he pulled her tight against his chest. He wasn't leaving. Why was he not leaving? Falon wondered as he rubbed circles in her back and let her cry. "You should not want me. I don't understand. Aidan, I'm not pure anymore. They..," Falon couldn't even finish. It had been so horrible in that prison. The things that they did to her still gave her nightmares. What they did to her was

219

unforgivable. She had gone into that prison an innocent child and had come out worn, scarred, and broken.

Aidan pulled back and cupped her face with his hands, "It wasn't your fault, Falon. Nothing that happened to you has been your fault. What happened to you in there...," Aidan stopped and took a breath as he tried to control the anger he was feeling. Not towards Falon, but towards his father and the ones that hurt her, "was not your fault. And I swear to you, that I'll make sure he pays for hurting you."

"But I'm a monster. And I'm.."

Aidan hushed her by covering her mouth with his. He poured into the kiss everything he felt for her. The love and passion that was unlike anything he had ever hoped for. When he pulled back, they were both breathless.

"Falon, nothing will ever change how I feel about you," Aidan brushed her tears away with his thumbs. "And you are the furthest thing from a monster. You have a pure heart, and you would do anything to help out anyone in need." Aidan scoffed, "Even if that means putting yourself in harm's way. Which we really are

220

going to have to work on. And the whole disappearing thing, I swear, you took a good three hundred years off my life when you disappeared for so long."

Falon found her first laugh in what seemed like forever, "I love you, Aidan."

Aidan wrapped his arms around her waist and pulled her tight against him, "And I love you. You have become the most important thing to me. I don't know what I would do if anything happened to you." He sighed and put his forehead to hers. "I have something to tell you as well."

"What is it?" Falon asked as he tightened his hold on her. It was as if he feared she'd disappear on him again.

"I...I helped kill the Elementals. I..."

"Aidan," Falon said softly as she pulled back enough to cup his face with her hands. "If I had been old enough, I would have to. They were evil and needed to be stopped. I just hope I don't turn out like them," she said as she dropped her hands and looked down instead of looking at Aidan.

Aidan grabbed Falon's chin and made her look at him. "You'll never be like them," he said remembering the prophecy that had been said over him so many years ago. After meeting Falon, he had decided that the prophecy was false, but now he knew the truth. His mate was a different kind of Fire Elemental, and she wasn't ever going to be the monster she thought she was. "I'll never let you be like that."

Falon looked up at him with tears in her eyes. "You won't?" she asked with a hope in her voice that was new to her.

"No, I won't. You will always be my Falon. You will never be a monster. Even when you start using your powers, you'll still be my Falon," Aidan said as he leaned forward and kissed away her tears. "You'll always be you."

"You promise?" Falon asked sounding more like a child than she ever had before. She knew she was being silly, but she also knew that if Aidan made a promise then it would be true.

"Yes, I promise."

Falon nodded then snuggled against his chest. "I still don't want to use my powers though, but I will if you're there with me and want me too."

"You need to use them, but we will worry about that later." Aidan let out a content sigh as his arms tightened around Falon, and he placed his chin on the top of her head. "Falon, will you..." Aidan cleared his throat, "will you be my mate for life? Will you...be joined with me?" he asked nervously. Why he was nervous all of sudden he didn't know.

"Yes. I would be honored," Falon said as she looked up at Aidan with a smile on her face. For the first time in years, she felt the weight of all that had happen to her lift off of her. It was as if Aidan had taken it all away. He had heard about her past and what she was, and he still wanted her. It was as if his love had pieced together her broken heart and made her whole again. She knew that the scars would always be there, but now, it seemed whole.

"Falon, I think we may have a problem though," Aidan said as he held her against his chest. He loved the feel of her against him.

"Hmm?" she asked content with just being in his arms. She laid her head back on his chest and took in his smell and the way she felt against him. They fit perfectly together.

"Your father hates me."

Falon laughed, "He will get over it. He's just worried about me."

"Are you sure?" Aidan asked the worry evident in his voice. He wouldn't have normally cared, but he wanted Falon's family to welcome him not reject him. Falon had been through enough pain in her life without there being family problems.

"Between Jonas and myself, we'll bring him around. Besides, Jonas likes you and that's all that matters to me." Falon moved her hand to cup the back of his neck then she brought his head down to hers.

Aidan captured her mouth with his. This was right. This was home.

Chapter Twelve

"Absolutely not!" Jeremiah yelled out as he tried to walk away from Jonas, Falon, and that man.

"Father, why not?" Falon asked as she stepped in front of him blocking his way.

"Because I won't have you tied to him," Jeremiah snapped out in disgust as he pointed at Aidan, "Falon, listen to me..."

"No, you listen," Falon demanded as she crossed her arms in front of her chest and stared her father down. "I love him, and I want to be with him. Why can you not just be happy for me?"

"His father..."

"His father has nothing to do with him. I want to be joined with Aidan not Damian," Falon interrupted yet again.

Jeremiah stood in front of his daughter. She had never been one to contradict him. If he said no, she went along with it. So why was she not now? Jeremiah knew the truth, and he didn't like it one bit. His baby girl was in love with the son of a monster. How could she want to be joined with him, knowing who his father was?

"Falon, if father won't preform the ceremony I will," Jonas said as he came over and put his arm around her shoulders. His little sister was finally happy, and he wasn't going to let anyone ruin that. Not even their father.

"You are not the head Fae here, so you can't," Jeremiah said smugly. And it was never going to happen. His baby was not going to marry the son of Damian. Never.

Aidan came over to stand next to Falon. He reached for her hand and laced his fingers with hers, "Sir, I love your daughter, and I won't do anything to harm her. I want to spend the rest of my life with her. She's my life and home."

"I..."

"Father, that's enough," Jonas said with a snap. "You won't deny my sister the right to be with her mate."

"Jonas, watch your tone. I won't approve of her marrying Aidan," Jeremiah said pointing at his son.

"Fine," Jonas said with a look towards Falon. "I guess, Falon, you and Aidan will just have to do things the old fashioned way. Before the bonding ceremony was created, Fae would just live together to prove that they were mates. That's what you will have to do now."

Falon looked at Jonas in shock. She couldn't believe her brother had just said that. He was always one for the ceremony and doing things right. She was the one who always tried to get around the rules. "I guess Jonas is right. If you refuse to do the ceremony, Aidan and I will just do what we have to do. I love him, and I plan to start living my life with him with or without the ceremony."

"Falon," Aidan tried to get Falon's attention, but she just squeezed his hand gently.

He wanted to be with her; if this was the only way then so be it, but he didn't want to cause strife in her family. He wanted Falon to have peace. She needed some peace in her life, dammit! And he was going to see that she got it.

"I guess that is the only option," Jonas said with a sad sigh as he looked as his father.

"I won't allow that!" Jeremiah said getting angrier than before.

"Then do the ceremony, Father," Jonas said as he crossed his arms over his chest.

Aidan saw the look of confidence on Jonas and Falon's faces, and it finally clicked what was going on. They were pushing Jeremiah into the ceremony. Aidan sighed sadly, "Falon, I won't let you do this to your father. I love you, but I won't cause friction with your family. You have had enough strife and war in your life without it being in your family. I want you to have peace, love."

Falon looked at Aidan. "Aidan, he will never except this," she said trying to get him to understand. The idea of not being with Aidan was almost causing her to become panicked.

She needed him, and she wasn't going to let him go.

Aidan touched her face gently to try and sooth her. He could tell just by looking at her that she was on the verge of losing control. "We just need to give him more time. I'll still be here with you. We'll just be taking things more slowly than we had thought. But I promise, I'm not leaving you." Telling Falon that he wasn't leaving her seemed to calm her down, but she still didn't look happy about the whole situation. He imagined he didn't look too thrilled about it either, but he knew that this was the right thing to do. He would just have to behave himself for a little while longer. Oh yeah, like that was going to be possible.

Jeremiah watched the two talk, and he saw the love that both of them felt for each other. It was hard not to. He rubbed the back of his neck, and finally, he admitted to himself the truth. It wasn't that Aidan was Damian's son. All anyone had to do was spend a few moments with Aidan to realize he was nothing like his father. It was the fact that this man had come in and taken his baby from him. Jeremiah looked at his daughter and realized that his baby was all grown up, and it was time for her to start a family of her own. Hanging on to her like this was only causing there to be riff between them that he didn't like. Jeremiah finally spoke, "Let's get this ceremony over with."

Aidan and Falon both turned and looked at Jeremiah in shock. "You'll do it?" Falon asked as she looked at her father.

"Yes. You two belong together, and I'm not going to be the one to destroy your happiness. I realize now that the only reason I was trying to stop it was because I felt like I was losing my baby, but now, I know the truth. I'm not losing you but gaining another son. Aidan, I'm sorry for the way I've been treating you. I know that you are nothing like your father. I only had to spend a few minutes with you to realize that, but," he said with fire in his eyes, "I promise you that if you hurt my daughter, I'll kill you."

"I understand," Aidan said trying not to smile, but he was so happy. In a few moments, Falon would be his.

Falon beamed with happiness as she threw her arms around her father's neck. "Thank you,

Daddy," Falon said into his neck then she kissed his cheek.

"You're welcome, my baby. Now let's begin," Jeremiah cleared his throat and started the ceremony.

~~~

"The council won't be happy about this," Jeremiah said as he watched Aidan and Falon head to their room after the ceremony was over. He had to admit, they did make a good looking couple. He was definitely going to get some beautiful grandchildren from them.

"They don't get to determine her life," Jonas said with a smile. "I'm overjoyed to see her so happy."

"As am I, but what if..."

"Let the what ifs worry about themselves," Jonas said with a smile. "I'm sure there will be plenty of them. Besides, I have heard nothing but good things about Aidan since returning home. It seems that he has made quite a few friends. And not just in the Fae.

"It's true. The boy has a good heart. All though, I don't think he would enjoy hearing that. I believe he likes for people to think he's mean." Jeremiah laughed, "Wouldn't he be upset if he found out that we all thought he was a big softy."

"Yes, he has a good heart, but don't doubt for a minute that if someone tried to threaten his friends or family he wouldn't turn into a cold, killing man. He wasn't the most feared bounty hunter for no reason. I'm also sure that once he sets his mind on a prize he can be quite persistent."

"I'm sure. I mean, look at how he captured Falon," Jeremiah said with a laugh that was joined by Jonas.

~~~

As they entered the room, Aidan quickly turned Falon so that she was facing him. How had he gotten so lucky? He guessed that for once in his life Fate had been working for him instead of against. "I love you, Falon."

"And I love you," Falon said right before Aidan's lips covered her own. She sighed as he wrapped his arms around her waist and pulled her tight to him. Okay for once she had to hand it to Fate. Fate definitely knew what it was doing this time.

"You're mine now. Always and Forever," Aidan said as he scooped her up into his arms and carried her over to the bed. As he laid her gently down in the center of the bed, he couldn't help but smile at how beautiful she was.

"And you're mine. Always and Forever," Falon said as he came down on top of her. Falon's eyes took in the look of Aidan. He was so handsome. She was about to tell him just that when he made her lose all thought by bringing his lips back to hers.

As the kiss intensified, Aidan used his Fae powers to make their clothes disappear. After which, they were both lost to the passion and love that consumed them. They were lost to the testament to love that was as old as time.

Chapter Thirteen

Aidan rolled over and reached for Falon only to find her space was empty. He quickly sat up and looked around the room. "Falon?" Aidan called out as he pushed the last of the sleepiness out of his mind. After her disappearing on him for four weeks, he began to panic. "Falon!"

"Here," Falon said as she came into the room carrying a tray of food. "I thought you might be hungry since we didn't get around to eating dinner last night."

Aidan sighed then smiled as Falon's face flushed with color. "Yeah I guess we didn't." Aidan sat up, and once Falon put the tray on the stand next to the bed, he pulled her down into the bed and rolled her onto her back. "Good morning," he said looking down at her with a smile on his face.

"Morning," Falon said with a laugh as she wrapped her arms around his neck. "You're in a playful mood this morning."

Aidan leaned down and kissed the side of her neck making Falon sigh. "Yes I am," he said before he brought his lips to hers. As the kiss deepened, they forgot all about the food and only thought about each other.

~~~

"We need to get up," Falon said as she rubbed Aidan's chest with her hand.

"Why?" Aidan asked as he grabbed two pieces of cheese off of the tray of food. He ate one and handed Falon the other.

"Because, I need to go train some of the guards, and you need to get to know everyone," Falon sat up and put her back to the headboard of the bed.

Aidan sat up and looked over at Falon. "Which means you want me to try to get everyone to like me?"

"Nope. They will come around once they get to know you. I just want you to meet everyone. Since my father is the head Fae, I kind of am....umm..."

Aidan sat up straighter than before. "That's why they call you My Lady. You're their princess."

"Yeah kind of. We aren't too big on ceremony here, but they are rather protective of me. They will want to get to know the Fae that won my heart," she said as she brushed a piece of hair out of his face.

Aidan smiled. "So I won your heart, did I?"

"Yes, you did." Falon stood up and wrapped herself in a robe. "So do I need to get you some clothes or..."

Before she could finish Aidan had changed into a pair of brown leather pants, and a white shirt. He looked amazing.

"Wow!" Falon came over to him and kissed him gently on the lips. "Now, I need to go change." She went to walk off, but before she got too far she found herself in a long dress.

"Very funny," she said sarcastically as she turned to look at Aidan.

"What? You look beautiful," Aidan said with an innocent look on his face. He smiled sweetly as he looked her up and down. He thought she looked amazing and decent, which is something he couldn't say about her regular outfits. The very idea of all these men seeing her in one of her regular outfits was driving him crazy.

"Aidan," Falon said warningly, "I can't fight in this, and I have training to do," she said as she glared at him.

"Fine," Aidan huffed and changed her into a pair of leather pants and a lose fitting black shirt that went past her butt. There was no reason for her to be showing off everything she had. "Better?"

"I guess asking for something a little tighter would be..."

"It is tight enough," Aidan growled as he pulled her into his arms. "I'm not keen on everyone seeing you in one of your normal outfits. I don't like the way their eyes roam you.

I should be the only one who looks at you that way."

"Very well, but eventually, you're going to have to let me go back to my normal clothing. I can't fight the enemy in this. They could grab a hold of the extra fabric and use it against me. That's why I wear the outfits I do." As she looked at him, she was shocked to see that he looked angry. "What's wrong now?"

"You're not going to be fighting any enemies. I...I won't lose you," Aidan said sternly. Just the thought of losing her was making him go into a panic. He couldn't lose her. He wouldn't lose her.

Falon raised an eyebrow at him, "I'll continue to fight for what is right, Aidan. You will have to get over it." Falon moved out of his arms and went to leave, but he stopped her.

"Falon, you..."

Falon cupped the back of his neck and pulled him down for an amazingly passionate kiss. As the kiss intensified, Aidan pushed her against the wall. When they pulled apart, they were both breathless.

"I trust you, now, I need you to trust me. I promise I'll take fewer chances than I did before, but I can't stop fighting."

Aidan put his forehead to hers. "Very well," he said repeating what she had said earlier. "But I'll be by your side."

Falon chuckled, "Of course. Come on." She grabbed his hand and led him out of the room. They headed down many halls and were greeted by a variety of people. Some were Humans, some Fae, and some Witches. Aidan noticed that the Fae were affectionate toward Falon while the other groups were just polite. "Where are we going?" Aidan asked as they turned another corner.

"We're going to where the Fae train. Not many do, but the ones who do come here," Falon said as she came to the end of one halls and pushed open the door. As they came into the room, Aidan was amazed at how large it was.

"Do you think Cale is here? I haven't seen him today," Aidan asked as he scanned the room. There were a few Fae in the room that he had already met, but there were more that he had not.

"I'm sure he's with Ariana, which means, he's with the Witches." Falon laughed as she saw the look on Aidan's face, "Don't worry they won't do anything to him."

"Are you sure? Fae and Witches haven't always gotten along," Aidan stated as he stared down a particularly young Fae who was staring at his wife.

"Yes, I'm sure. The groups here get along. Besides, no one would dare touch the mate of the Witch princess." Falon looked around the room and saw Jarus and Tomas. "Come, we will work with Jarus and Tomas. It is my duty to teach them, and their duty to teach everyone else."

Aidan followed closely behind Falon as they made their way towards the two guards.

"My Lady, do we get the great honor of you joining us today?" Jarus asked as he bowed before Falon, took her hand, and kissed the top of it.

Aidan felt like his body temperature had just jumped up as anger filled him. How dare this Fae touch his Falon! He was about to say that very thing when Falon removed her hand and laughed.

"You, my friend, are not as charming as you think," Falon said as she looked at her guards and friends.

"I keep telling him that, My Lady, but he refuses to listen," Tomas said as he bowed to Falon. When he caught her eye, he winked at her. "Now I, on the other hand, am quiet charming."

"Oh, you are, are you?" Falon asked with a smile. These two Fae had been her friends for as long as she could remember. They were loyal, good soldiers, and huge flirts. Falon had grown accustomed to it over the years, and she didn't even think about what it was doing to Aidan.

Aidan looked at Falon, and his frown deepened. She was encouraging this ridiculous behavior. "Falon," Aidan said warningly.

Falon turned her attention to Aidan, and her smile faded as she saw the serious look on his face. "What is the problem?" Had something happened that she hadn't seen?

"What is the problem?" Aidan asked repeating the question back to her, "The problem is *my wife* is flirting with other men," he said stressing the *my wife* part.

Falon raised an eyebrow at Aidan then turned back towards Jarus and Tomas. "Guys, this is my husband Aidan. You met him once before, but I thought I would officially introduce him. Aidan," she said turning towards her husband, "these are my friends and head guards, Jarus and Tomas. They're big flirts, but they don't mean anything by it. Actually, they would flirt with a wall if you give them time."

"Hey, would not," Tomas said as he crossed his arms in front of his chest and acted like he was offended. He wasn't, but it was fun to act.

"I won't lie. I would," Jarus said as he put out his hand for Aidan to shake. "I'll probably flirt with you if you give me time."

Everyone laughed.

Aidan looked at the hand and reached out to shake it. Some of the tension from earlier easing as he came to terms with the fact that these Fae were Falon's friends, nothing more.

"Anyway, are we going to fight or continue talking?" Falon asked as she looked at the three.

"Fight," they all said together. They were heading to the mat when Tomas looked at Falon's clothing. He had never seen her wear something so loose. He then looked at Aidan and saw how his eyes kept scanning the room. The man was extremely jealous. Tomas chuckled to himself evilly. This could be a lot of fun.

"What was that laugh about?" Falon asked quietly. She knew her friend, and she knew that when he laughed like that he was up to something.

"Nothing," Tomas said as he looked down at Falon.

Falon narrowed her eyes at him trying to figure out what exactly he was up to, but before she had it figured out, Aidan captured her attention.

"Falon, are you going to fight with me or..," Aidan stopped when Falon's clothes changed all of sudden. He looked at her with a grim expression on his face as he saw her in her normal outfit except for this one was a lot tighter. "What the hell are you wearing?"

Falon looked down at her clothes. "What the hell happened to my clothes?" she looked up and glared at Tomas. "What do you think you're doing?"

Aidan's eyes jerked towards Tomas. "You did this?" he asked as he took a step closer to Tomas. Aidan waved his hand towards Falon causing her clothes to change back.

"How did I get involved in this?" Falon asked as she crossed her arms in front of her chest.

"What's wrong you don't like seeing our Lady in her regular clothes?" Tomas asked as he stepped closer to Aidan. "We helped her pick them out," Tomas said with a cocky smile, "Just think they could be a lot worse." At that moment Falon's clothes changed again.

Falon looked down and groaned, Jarus was laughing so hard he was crying, Aidan was growling, Tomas was looking smug, and ever Fae in the room was now looking at Falon. Lucky for her, there weren't that many Fae who actually trained. Only the guards were allowed to so that was all that was there. Of course, that didn't help with Falon's embarrassment or the fact that every bloody being in the city would know about this by night fall. Falon closed her eyes as the embarrassment took hold. She was in a dress that barely covered her butt and cut so low that you could see a lot of her breasts. This couldn't get any worse.

Aidan was struggling with his anger and enjoying the view of his wife in that dress. Of course, after he took his eyes off of her and looked around the room his anger won out. He quickly changed her short dress into a long one that covered everything. And I mean everything. "Stop changing her clothes," he yelled.

"Stop trying to make her into something she isn't. She's not going to decide to take one of us to her bed."

"I know that!" Aidan said as he looked at the man in front of him. "I never thought she was!"

Falon looked at the two men who were standing toe to toe and shook her head. She quickly turned on her heels and left the room. If those two idiots wanted to fight this thing out, then they could do it without dragging her into it. She mumbled under her breath as she left the room.

"Good, because the way you were acting was making me think that you might have that impression of her. I can assure you that no Fae here will take advantage of our Lady. She is our leader and friend. Stop being so overprotective and jealous. Besides, if anyone touched her that she did not want to touch her, they would be dead." Tomas said as he went to walk off.

"And who would kill them since you think I'm being over protective?" Aidan asked with his arms crossed. She was his wife, he had the right to be overprotective and jealous.

"She would," Tomas said with a smile.

Aidan looked around to see all the Fae in the room nodding in agreement.

"Umm...not to interrupt this very interesting conversation, but the person that this whole thing was about has left the room. And I believe she was not happy," Jarus said looking at Aidan with a smirk.

Aidan looked around the room and then looked back at Jarus. "How angry was she?" he asked nervously.

"She looked like she was ready to catch fire," Jarus said with a wink. "I suggest you be prepared when you go to her."

Aidan rubbed the back of his neck and headed out of the room. He listened as all the Fae in the training room burst into laughter. Aidan swore under his breath then headed for his and Falon's room.

~~~

Falon came into the room, locked the door, and changed her own bloody clothes. "What the hell is all these men's problem?" she yelled out as she fell back onto the bed. She put her arm over her eyes and sighed deeply. As she laid there thinking about her husband and wondering why he was so jealous, she heard the doorknob jiggle.

"Falon, unlock the door," Aidan said as he looked at the door that separated him from his wife. He was in deep trouble if she was locking him out. "Please," he added hoping that she would let him in if he sounded nice instead of jealous. He couldn't help it. When he saw another man staring at her, something in him wanted to come out and strangle that man. Aidan pinched the bridge of his nose trying to understand what had happened to him. Hell, he knew what had happened to him. Falon happened to him. She turned him into a jealous, overprotective Fae. And did he mention crazy.

"Why?" Falon asked as she slowly sat up.

"I..," Aidan ran his hand through his hair, "I need to talk to you."

Falon got up and went over to the door. Once it was open, she stood in the way so that Aidan couldn't get it. "Yes?" she asked as she leaned against the door jamb and crossed her arms in front of her chest.

"Can I not come into my own room?" Aidan asked with a raised eyebrow.

Falon moved aside and motioned with her hand for him to enter. "Aidan, I'm not angry at you if that is what you are worried about," she said as she moved to sit on the bed. "Tomas is the one who started the whole mess." Falon narrowed her eyes then fell back on the bed, "And I plan on having a word with him about it. I just needed some time alone. To...try and figure out some things."

"Falon, he was proving a point. I was so jealous that I wasn't letting you be you, and I'm sorry for that," Aidan said as he laid down on the bed next to his wife. He looked at her with a sad smile on his face. "Do you forgive me?" he asked as he brushed a piece of hair out of her face.

"There is nothing to forgive. I'm sure I'll have my jealous moments. I hope I handle them better, but we will see I am sure," Falon said with a small smile. "However, I want you to know that I don't like being put into the middle of one of your disagreements." Falon's smile faded, "I definitely didn't like being put into either of those dresses, but I have to admit yours was not near as bad as Tomas."

Aidan chuckled, "I'll remember not to involve you like that again." Aidan leaned over her so that his head was mere inches from hers. "About the dress?"

"Yes?" Falon asked her voice turning husky sounding from the nearness of her husband.

Aidan smiled mischievously at Falon. "I really, really liked you in it." He moved his head to the side and nuzzled Falon's neck.

Falon wrapped her hand in Aidan's hair as he kissed and nipped at her neck. "Aidan, clothes," Falon said breathlessly.

Aidan leaned up and looked into Falon's eyes. His smile increased when he changed Falon into the dress that Tomas had come up with earlier.

"Aidan!" Falon yelled as she looked at her clothes. She quickly moved out from under Aidan, stood up, and put her hands on her hips. "Change me out of this. Now!" she said as she glared down at her husband.

Aidan rolled to his back, put his hands behind his head, and smiled up at her. "I like it."

Falon watched as his eyes started at her face and slowly made their way down her body. "You like it?" she asked in a shocked voice, "But you had a fit when Tomas put me in it earlier."

Aidan jumped up from the bed, grabbed Falon, and pulled her down onto the bed before Falon could even react. As Aidan rolled her onto her back, a squeal and a laugh escaped from Falon. "I didn't like everyone else seeing you in it. My eyes are the only eyes that I want to ever see this much of you," he said as his hand and eyes moved down her body. "You're so beautiful."

Falon closed her eyes as Aidan's touch set her on fire. "Aidan, please."

Aidan brought his mouth down to Falon's and gave into her plea with his own.

Chapter Fourteen

Aidan opened his eyes as he heard the knock at the door. "Go away," he said loudly as he rolled over and pulled Falon to him. Once she was in his arms, he started to fall back to sleep. He was almost there when another knock sounded at the door. "I swear if it's Cale, at this early hour, I'm going to kill him," he said as he jerked the covers back and got out of bed. He quickly put on a pair of pants as he stomped across the room.

"Could you be any louder?" Falon asked as she snuggled back under the blankets.

"I'm not the one knocking on the door," Aidan said with a snap.

"Shout at them not me. I didn't do anything," Falon said from under the mounds of blankets. She knew she should probably get up and save whoever was at the door, but she just couldn't find the energy. It was only around four in the morning, and she was not a morning person. She smirked as she realized that neither was her husband.

"What?!" Aidan yelled as he jerked open the door. His eyes went wide in shock as he saw Jeremiah staring at him on the other side of the door.

"Not a morning person I see," Jeremiah said trying not to laugh. "I apologize for the intrusion, but the council is requesting your and Falon's presence. Immediately."

Aidan ran his hand over his face trying to wake himself up. "Why so early?"

"They scheduled the meeting as soon as they were informed of two unions. Apparently, Timothy had been keeping Cale and Ariana's a secret. I think maybe I should have as well, but I was excited for you two. Anyway, they're now wanting to have a meeting to discuss these two relationships," Jeremiah said with a raised eyebrow hoping that Aidan understood the severity of the situation. He did not want his new son-in-law going into that room unprepared. There was a good possibility that the council will want the two unions dissolved, and if they are not, there's no telling what the council will do.

"There is nothing to discuss. Falon is mine," Aidan said in a growl understanding fully what Jeremiah was saying. No one was going to take her away from him.

"I understand that, but you won't be able to handle this with force. I need you to be in control."

"Why?" Aidan asked with confusion. Why should he be in control? "If someone was trying to take your mate from you, would you be calm?"

"No, but my mate, Emily, was a very calm individual. When I would go off on a tangent, she would be there calming me down. I fear that out of the two of you," Jeremiah said looking at Aidan then waving towards the room, "you will have to be the one to use your head. Once Falon finds out why this meeting has been called, she won't be happy. If she believes that they will take you from her she will fight and not think about it. It will be instinctive, and Falon's instincts are a tad dangerous. Do you understand now why you have to be the calm one?"

"I see your point, but I won't let Falon be taken from me either."

"I know, Aidan. Just keep her from doing anything stupid, and I'll do the rest." Jeremiah waited until Aidan nodded at him, "Good, now get her up and come to the council room." Jeremiah then left leaving Aidan alone to get Falon up.

Aidan closed the door and went over to where Falon was snuggled under the covers. He was about to wake her up when she spoke.

"I know, I have to get up and not do anything stupid. Isn't that correct?" Falon asked without coming out from under the blankets.

Aidan rubbed the back of his neck then pulled the covers back until he could see Falon's face. "You heard all of that, did you?" he asked as he saw her face. He looked into her eyes and noticed that they were starting to get a little red in them.

"Yes, I heard it," Falon said as she sat up and headed for the bathroom. "You're supposed to keep me from doing anything stupid when the idiots try and tell me that we can't be together. Is that the gist of the conversation?" she asked as she turned the water on.

"Falon, your father is just worried that one of us will do something that will make the matter worse," Aidan said trying to remain calm, but honestly, he was having a hard time with it. He didn't like having to be calm any more than she did, but at least, he had complete control of his powers. If something happened, he meant it to happen, but if something happened with Falon's powers, she may not be meaning to.

Falon came over to him. "You won't have to keep me from doing anything stupid. I hope," she said calming down a bit. "Listen, I'm going to get cleaned up then I'll be ready to go." She kissed Aidan gently on the lips. She was about to pull back when Aidan wrapped his hand in her hair and held her in place as he deepened the kiss.

All of Aidan's anger fell away as he kissed his wife and pushed her towards the bathroom. "I think I'll join you," he said right before he shut the bathroom door, keeping the rest of the world out for just a little longer.

~~~

"You two are late," Jeremiah said with a smirk.

Falon avoided looking at her father as Aidan put his arm possessively around her waist.

"I had trouble getting Falon to leave the bathroom this morning."

Falon jerked her head around and looked at Aidan evilly. "I wasn't the only one who had trouble this morning," she said through a clenched teeth. Her glare told Aidan how much she really disliked him at the moment.

Aidan just looked into her eyes and winked at her. He then squeezed her waist a little to let her know that it was harmless fun. Falon finally just shook her head and looked up at the council trying not to laugh at the looks on all of their faces.

Jeremiah laughed. "Young love," he mumbled under his breath then looked at the rest of the council members. "Now that we are all here, I believe we should begin."

"Yes, I believe that the sooner we get this over with the sooner we can get down to more important business," Timothy said with an annoyed tone.

"This is a serious situation, and it will be treated as such," a Fae council member said as he stood up and glared at the two couples before him.

"This is not a council matter. This is a family matter, Daniel," Jeremiah said with a snap to his voice.

"No, this is a council matter," Jonathan said as he stood up.

"What the hell is he doing here?!" Aidan asked as he pushed Falon behind his back. Images of Falon falling in his arms not breathing entered his mind. "He tried to kill

MY WIFE!" Aidan shouted as he looked around at the council members.

Falon grabbed Aidan's arm. "Calm down, Love," she said softly. And her father was worried about her doing something stupid. "I'm sure there is a rational explanation," she said as she looked at the council.

Timothy gave Falon a sympathetic look. "The council decided that Jonathan should be back on the council. They believe that it was just the shock of seeing Aidan that caused Jonathan to behave the way he did. He has been given a second chance."

"He almost killed Falon!" Ariana shouted.

"I didn't mean her any harm. I was aiming at Aidan," Jonathan said with a sneer as he looked at the two couples. If everything went the way he hoped, Aidan and Cale would be gone from this city by nightfall, and hopefully, Ariana and Falon with them. For years, both of them had been fighting against him and all he wanted to do. Finally, he would be rid of them and all his plans would fall into place.

"If the council decided that Jonathan should be back, then we should respect it," Falon said calmly as she looked at her friends. To be honest, she wanted to be angry with the council for this, but she knew that there were more important matters for them to discuss.

"Thank you, Falon," Aaron, one of the other Witch council members, said with a small smile.

"Yes, thank you," Benjamin, the leader of the Humans, said with a nod of his head.

Good, she had at least four out of twelve on their side now. Falon thought as she looked at the other council members. She looked at the Humans and saw that Eric, Peter, and Travis were nodding their heads at her. Well, she at least had the Humans on their side, that was good. Now, she just needed the other Fae and Witches. She looked over at the Fae and saw that Daniel was frowning at her. Okay that was one against them. She then turned her eyes towards the other three. She knew that her father was with them, but she wasn't for sure about Nathaniel and Abel. Falon finally turned her eyes to the Witches, and only Timothy looked like he was on their side. This was going to be an interesting meeting. "I believe the council has called this meeting to discuss my relationship with Aidan and Ariana's relationship with Cale," Falon said with a calm, steady voice.

Aidan laced his fingers with Falon's and looked down at her. He had been the one who was supposed to be calm. Well, he had failed at that miserably. At least Falon was keeping her head on straight. He looked at Cale and Ariana and saw that they weren't any happier about this than he was. Aidan looked down at Falon as she squeezed his hand. He squeezed back reassuring her that everything was going to be all right.

"Yes, let's get down to the situation at hand," Timothy said as he motioned for all the members to take their seats. "The council believes that you and Ariana should have consulted us before having the bonding ceremony that joined each of you with these Fae."

"Why?" Falon asked in a voice that sounded only mildly curious.

"It's the way of things," Jonathan said in a hiss.

"When did it become the way of things? Last I checked, the council has never taken an interest in who had a bonding ceremony. So, why are you taking an interest in Ariana and mine?"

"You're the leader of the Fae's daughter, and Ariana is the leader of the Witch's daughter. Different standards are to be held for you," Jonathan said getting louder than he had been earlier. The hold he had on his anger was slipping away little by little.

Falon looked around at the groups and saw a few nod. "All right then, why did Jonas not come before the council when he had his ceremony?"

"We didn't deem it necessary at the time," Jonathan snapped.

"Very well. Then, what you are telling me is that you don't trust Ariana and me. I don't understand this. We have never given you a reason to not trust our judgment. So, why are you not trusting us now?" Falon asked as she looked calmly at the council members. She then looked at Aidan, Ariana, and Cale out of the corners of her eyes. She saw that they were all looking at her in shock. Why was it so shocking? She could be calm and behave when she needed to. She was going to have to talk to her friends and family when this was over with. Falon frowned as she thought about their lack of faith in her.

Jeremiah looked at his daughter and almost laughed. She had walked Jonathan right it to that one. Good for her.

Aidan was filled with a mixture of pride and worry. He was filled with pride because his wife was making a fool out of the Witch that had it in for them all. He was filled with worry because the Witch was beginning to look more and more dangerous. Aidan kept his eyes on the Witch waiting for any sign that he was going to hurt Falon. If he did, then no matter the consequence, he was going to kill him.

Timothy was trying hard not to laugh as he looked at all the faces of the council. They had definitely not been expecting Falon to use logic in her argument. They all, even him, had expected her to lose her temper which would have played right into Jonathan's hands.

"She is correct. We did not interfere with Jonas' bonding ceremony nor have we ever interfered. Aidan and Cale have done nothing to cause us concern and Falon and Ariana have always had the Fae's trust," Daniel said coming around to Falon's side. It would look bad if he did not show his trust in his Lady, and truth be told she was one of the only people that he always trusted. Daniel shook his head in aggravation, he shouldn't have listened to Jonathan. Why had he anyway? For some reason, he had listened to the lies Jonathan had been telling the council. He didn't even like Jonathan, but for some reason, his arguments had made sense. Daniel began to wonder why that was true when Jonathan stood up with so much anger that it poured off him in waves. Waves that were filling the entire room.

"Why do you so easily turn to her side?!" Jonathan shouted. He turned and glared at Falon.

Falon braced herself for whatever Jonathan was going to throw at her, but what he said almost had her staggering backwards.

"Are you one of her conquest?" He asked his voice coming out in disgust. "Did this whore win your quick approval through her bed?"

Falon's mouth fell open, and her hand tightened on Aidan's. "Aidan, don't do anything stupid," she said softly her voice coming out strained. Why did every insist on calling her a whore? What had she ever done to give that impression?

Aidan was shaking he was so mad. He looked towards Jeremiah, but all he got was a shake of the head. What the hell?! He couldn't just stand here and let that man talk about his wife this way. No one had the right to talk about his woman like that.

Falon let go of Aidan's hand and wrapped her arm around his waist. After he wrapped his arm around her shoulders, she placed her head against his shoulder. "It will be all right," she said for his ears only.

"You need to watch how you speak about my daughter, Jonathan," Jeremiah said as he stood up and stared down Jonathan.

"And the way you speak to other council members," Daniel said as he joined Jeremiah in standing.

Timothy stood to his feet, and was followed by the rest of the Witch's council. "I believe that you have said enough, Jonathan. I think it was a mistake for us to allow you to rejoin the council."

"Agreed," the rest of the council said in unison.

"It creeps me out when they do that," Falon said to Aidan.

Aidan relaxed a little and let a small chuckle escape him. "Have I told you how much I love you?" he asked quietly as he looked down at his beautiful wife.

"Not today," Falon said, her smile brightening.

Aidan was about to lean down and kiss Falon in front of everyone when Jonathan yelled out.

"You! This is your fault!" Jonathan screamed as he pointed at Ariana.

Aidan was taken back, by the fact that Jonathan was pointing at Ariana, not Falon.

Falon moved away from Aidan before he could grab her and took her place next to Ariana. "Back off," Falon said her voice going from calm to deadly in a matter of seconds. She may have been able to remain calm while they talk to her, but no one talked to Ariana in a threatening manner.

"I'm not the one who was using an incantation to sway the minds of the other council members. I put everything back in balance," Ariana said as she looked around the room. "Some of you are feeling like Jonathan put ideas in your head. You're not understanding how you were swayed by him," she stated, her voice precise and clear.

Aidan watched in shock as most of the council members nodded their heads. What the hell was going on?

"We all know Jonathan is a powerful Witch, but I don't know if he is capable of that,"

Timothy said as he looked at his daughter with a look of confusion on his face.

"You...," Jonathan sputtered out. He tried taking a calming breath, but it didn't work. "How could I even do something like that? I'm not that powerful."

Falon looked at Ariana and then back towards the council. "I believe Ariana is telling the truth, but if you have your doubts, then there is a simple way to find out," she said as she turned her full attention to Jonathan. She watched as Jonathan's face paled and he started looking like a trapped rat. "May I?" Falon asked the council, but she never took her eyes off of Jonathan.

Aidan looked at his wife then back at Jonathan. As he looked at the Witch, a chill went down his spine. Something bad was about to happen; he could feel it.

"I agree," Jeremiah said as he looked around the room. "Let Falon find out the truth."

"No, I won't let...let that thing touch me!" Jonathan yelled as he took a step away from the group. If she searched out the truth in him then he was doomed. He couldn't allow this to happen.

"She is the Lady of the Fae, and you will show her respect!" Ariana shouted. "If you have nothing to hide, then you should not mind her searching for the truth."

Aidan looked at Falon then turned his attention to Ariana. "How will Falon find out the truth?" he asked as he looked around the room.

"I was wondering the same thing," Cale said as he leaned over and whispered to Aidan.

"A powerful incantation," Falon said as she touched her Witch's stone. "Now, will you allow me to find out the truth or not?" she asked as she looked at Jonathan.

Jonathan knew that his time was up. "I'll kill you all!" he yelled then everyone watched in shock as he pulled out a blue Witch's stone and released a bright blue flame into the room.

"What the hell is that?!" Aidan yelled as he pulled Falon back from the flame that was trying to make its way towards them.

"The door," Jeremiah yelled out as they headed to the door.

Aidan and the others tried with all their powers to open the door, but somehow Jonathan was keeping the door locked, and no amount of power was opening the door.

Falon turned her head to see Ariana trying to use her power to stop the flame. "Ariana, NO!" she yelled as the flame neared her friend. Falon tried to go to her, but Aidan grabbed her by the waist pulling her to him. "Let me go! I have to help her!" she screamed and fought against her husband, but he wouldn't let her go.

"No, you stay with me!" Aidan yelled as he watched half of the council members try and put out the flame and the others try to open the door. Aidan wanted to help, but all he could do was hold onto his wife. If he let her go, she would go head first into that flame. He just knew it.

Aidan looked away from Falon and saw Cale grab a hold of Ariana, but it was too late.

As Cale's arms wrapped around Ariana's waist, Jonathan moved his hand towards them causing the fire to consume them, laughing manically the whole time.

"Cale! Ariana!" Aidan yelled out as he watched his friends fall lifelessly to the floor. As Aidan looked at them, he couldn't see any burn marks, all he could see were their lifeless eyes staring at him from where they fell.

"Ariana! Cale! No!" Falon yelled out as she fought against Aidan. She then watched as Nathaniel, Travis, and Abel fell dead to the floor as the fire consumed them as well. "Aidan, let me go! I have to stop it! I have to stop Jonathan!"

"No, I'm getting you out of here!" Aidan said as he grabbed her and shoved her against the wall. He then turned, pressed his back to her, and looked over at Jeremiah and Timothy. His heart broke for Timothy. As Aidan watched him, he saw that Timothy's eyes kept returning to the face of his lifeless daughter. His heart broke as well as he saw his best friend lying on the floor dead. Aidan turned his eyes back to the flame and watched as it got closer. He knew that if they didn't get out soon they were all going to be dead.

"Aidan, let me go. I'm the Fire Elemental. I may be able to stop it!" Falon yelled as she shoved on Aidan's shoulder trying to get him to move. He was pressed so tightly to her she couldn't move.

"No, I won't watch you die!" Aidan yelled back as he turned and pulled her into his arms. "I won't watch you die," he said softly as he held her. He knew that they were out of time. He knew that they were both going to die soon, but he also knew that they would go together. Neither one of them would have to watch the other die. "It will be all right, My Love. I promise," he said softly as he touched her face with his hand.

Falon cupped Aidan's face with her hands, "I can stop this. I know I can," she pulled his face down to hers and kissed him with more passion than most feel in a life time. "I'm so sorry," she said as she pulled back from him and looked over at her father and Timothy. "Dad!" she yelled then suddenly Jeremiah and

Timothy were pulling Aidan away from Falon. Falon watched as Aidan kicked and fought trying to pull away from them to get to her, but he was unable to.

Falon looked away from her husband and met Jonathan's eyes. She pulled her power and took a step towards the blue fire that was making its way towards the rest of the people in the room. She brought her own fire to life forcing it to come out of her hands.

As Falon raised her fired up hands, she started pushing her fire towards Jonathan's fire. Slowly, she took a step forward pushing the blue flames back with her red ones. As she pushed, she realized that she wasn't going to be able to stop this fire like she had others. It was just too strong. It was almost as if it had its own life force which was making it stronger than anything she had ever faced before. On top of that, she hadn't used her power in so long that her fire was not as powerful as this fire.

Falon closed her eyes as she felt the fire pull at her. It was as if the blue flames were trying to reach out and tell her what to do. She listened careful to the power that was pulsing through her body, through her very veins.

273

Finally, she knew, but she didn't know how, that the only way to get control was to become one with the fire, letting her body absorb the flames, the energy. Falon opened her eyes, and she knew what she had to do. This was so going to suck.

Aidan fought against the hands and power that were holding him back. At first, it had just been Jeremiah and Timothy, but now all the remaining members of the council were holding onto him. "Let me go! Falon!" he screamed as he watched his wife, his love, move closer to the flames that had consumed Cale and Ariana. He couldn't watch her die. He would rather die than have to watch her sacrifice herself for them. "Falon!"

"Aidan, she is the only one who stands a chance of stopping this. Please, let her do this," Jeremiah yelled out trying to get over Aidan's screams and the laugh that Jonathan was giving off. He didn't want his daughter to do this, but he knew that if anyone could get control of this fire it would be Falon. If anyone could survive it's deadly touch it would be his daughter.

Aidan knew what he said was true, but he couldn't do it. He had to keep her safe. If he lost her, he would have nothing left. He would have nothing worth fighting for, nothing to keep him going. "Falon, please stop!" he begged hoping that his pleas would reach his wife. As he watched her fight, he wondered if she could even hear him or if she had given into her power completely. He was losing her to the power he promised to protect her from. *Please, Fate, don't be so cruel as to take her away,* Aidan pleaded in his mind over and over again. Fate couldn't be that cruel.

Falon heard her husband's pleas, but she knew that she couldn't stop. If she stopped, the few that were still alive in this room would be dead. Knowing what to do, Falon looked up and met Jonathan's eyes. "My life for theirs," she said loudly, then she dropped her hands and let the blue flames consume her. As the flames consumed her, she felt it entering her body with such a force that her mind couldn't comprehend what was happening to her. She felt herself bend over as the pain over took her then everything went black.

Chapter Fifteen

Aidan felt the blood drain from him as he watched as his wife, his life, allow the blue flame to consume her. "Falon! Dammit, Falon!" he shouted as he fought against the ones holding him.

Suddenly, the fight left him, and his knees gave out from under him. He hit the ground the hands that were holding him back letting him go. "Falon," he said softly his voice breaking as he hung his head. Fate had brought her into his life only to take her away from him.

Aidan looked up with every intention of getting up, and heading into the blue flames, when he saw his wife standing in the middle of the room. The blue flames wrapped around her until they disappeared into her skin. He watched as she looked down at her hands and the rest of her body as if she was confused about what had happened. Aidan slowly stood up, taking in her appearance as he did. She looked like she was glowing blue, like the flames that had consumed her.

"What is all this drama?" glowing blue Falon asked, her voice coming out in a mellow tone, as she put one hand on her hip and used her other to wave about in a very flowy manner.

Aidan looked at his wife in shock. "Falon?" he asked unsure of what was happening to his wife. Her skin was still glowing blue, and she was talking like she had consumed some kind of drug. Her normal stance had turned into the most relaxed stance he had ever seen.

Glowing blue Falon turned around to look at the man speaking to her. "Falon is not here at the moment, but she will be back shortly, darlin," she said with a wink. She turned back to look at the Witch who had conjured her up. "You!" she said with her finger pointing at the Witch with her necklace on. "You used me to hurt people. I'm not all about that. You're really harshing my mellow, man."

Aidan looked at his wife, or what looked like his wife, in shock. She looked like Falon, but she didn't act or sound like his wife. Of course, she was also glowing blue, and her eyes looked like the blue flames that had consumed her. "What has happened to my wife?!" he yelled as he took a step towards the woman that was supposed to be his wife.

"Listen, good lookin, I'll be with you in a moment," glowing blue Falon said as she looked at Aidan with a sexy smile on her face.

Usually, Aidan only saw that kind of smile, on his wife's face, in the bedroom. He shook his head as he watched her turn back around to face Jonathan.

"Now where was I? Oh yes," she said her smile fading, and her gaze growing heated with anger as she looked at Jonathan. "You used me to hurt others. I'm a lover not a fighter," she said as she looked over her shoulder and gave Aidan another wink. "I was never for violence, and I won't stand by it now. If it wasn't for this," she said turning her attention back to Jonathan and waving her hand up and down her body, "woman you would have killed everyone in this room and for want of more power," she said with a scoff. "And power from Damian is never a good thing." She shook her head sadly. "He only wants more power for himself, not for anyone else. As soon as would have finished what he demanded of you he would have disposed of you. I hope you learn from this," she said as she waved her hand, and with little power, the Witch's stone left Jonathan's neck and slowly came to be in Falon's hand. "This is mine, and I don't like it in someone's hands who upset my cool charm."

As the necklace left Jonathan's neck Falon waved her hand again causing Jonathan to fall to the floor. Suddenly, a scream of anger came out of Jonathan. "You took my powers! Give them back!"

"No, if you can't help people with your powers then you don't need them. Now, this being," she said as she motioned to her body again, "uses her powers for good, and she will do great things. You on the other hand will be doing nothing but messing with everyone's flow. If I was a person who killed, I would kill you. You're lucky that I'm against all that harsh treatment. You totally cause too much drama."

Aidan's mouth fell open as Falon turned to look at him and walked, or rather prissed, over to him, her hips swaying with ever step. She was walking so girly. This whole thing was weird. When Falon stood in front of him, Aidan watched her eyes roam up and down him.

"She chose well," she said in a purr that made Aidan uncomfortable. He moved his upper body back away from Falon as she moved in closer licking her lips as she did. "Real well."

"Can I have my wife back now?" he asked as he placed a hand out in front of him to keep her from getting any closer. It was one thing for his Falon to get in his space, but this was not his Falon. Aidan was so confused and unsure about this whole thing. Was she hitting on him? Was this being that was using Falon's body actually hitting on him? This was just weird. Falon was straight and to the point, it was one of the things he liked about his wife. This flirting was just weird coming from his wife.

"Yes, soon, but first I must fix the trouble this man caused," she said waving towards Jonathan. Falon winked at Aidan then turned and waved her hand around the room. As she released her powers a blue smoke wrapped itself around the bodies that were laying lifelessly on the floor.

Everyone watched in shock as the bodies started breathing and suddenly, they all sat up and looked around in confusion.

"What...what happened?" Ariana asked as she looked at Falon. "Falon?" she asked in confusion as she noticed the blue glow to her friend's skin and the blue of her eyes.

"Not at the moment, but soon. You're a powerful Witch, but you have the potential to be even more powerful. Soon you will become all you were meant to be," Falon said then she turned her attention on Cale. "Watch out for her and never leave her side. She will need you in the battle to come."

Cale nodded his head then looked at Aidan who was staring at all of them in disbelief. "Why are you looking at us that way?"

"You were dead. I mean really dead," Aidan said his voice hoarse with emotion. He refused to cry as the emotions within him built.

"Oh," is all Cale managed to say before everyone's attention was back on Falon.

"Who are you?" Aidan asked as he stared into the blue eyes that looked at him from Falon's face.

"I'll be whoever you want me to be, Sweetheart."

"Umm...how about a name?" Aidan asked uncomfortably. It was just weird watching his wife act like this. He wanted his Falon back, and he wanted her back now.

Glowing blue Falon pouted. "Very well. You can call me Witch's Fire for now. Now, give Falon a message for me. Tell her thank you and to keep this necklace safe for me. I'll be back to help her later. For now, my time here is done."

"Wait, what do you mean?" Ariana asked as she stood up and looked at the body of her friend.

"In time all will be revealed, Little Seer. For now, I'm going to go enjoy my freedom, but soon you will all see me again. Now peace and to you, gorgeous, lots of love," she said the last part to Aidan then the blue glow left Falon's body.

Aidan was barely able to catch Falon before she hit the floor in an unconscious heap. "Falon, baby, look at me," he demanded as he cradled her gently in his arms. His panic began to grow as she remained unresponsive in his arms.

"Go lay her down. I'm sure having such a powerful being in her body has warn her out," Jeremiah said speaking for the first time since Witch's Fire had taken over Falon's body.

Aidan looked over at Jonathan evilly, but his attention was turned when Falon groaned in his arms. It sounded like she was in pain.

"Go, Aidan, we will take care of that," Timothy said with more anger in his voice than anyone had ever heard before as his eyes looked at Jonathan.

"Find out about Damian. We need to know his plans," Aidan commanded as he stood up with Falon in his arms.

"We will. Go take care of Falon," Ariana said as she turned from Aidan and looked at Jonathan. "I believe I'll try my hand at Falon's incantation," she sneered. "Of course, if I fail it will cause you to be in extreme pain. Oh well, we do what we must," she said nonchalantly as she moved towards Jonathan.

"That's my wife," Cale proudly boasted to Aidan. "Go, Aidan, tend to your wife," he said as he put his hand on his friend's shoulder. "We will handle everything here."

Aidan watched as Cale walked over to stand next to Ariana. He nodded then abruptly left the room to look for Jonas. Everything else could wait until Jonas examined Falon and told Aidan she was going to be just fine. There was no telling what Witch's Fire had done to Falon's body, and Aidan wasn't going to rest until Jonas had looked her over, and Falon was awake, talking to him as her. He needed to hear her voice.

Aidan had a shiver pass through him as he thought about how Falon had been a few moments ago. It had just been too weird. He liked his Falon the way she was, and he hoped he would never again have to deal with Witch's

Fire. He shook his head as he thought about all Witch's Fire had said. A groan escaped him as he admitted to himself that he would have to see her again. However, maybe next time she would go into someone else, instead of his wife.

"What happened?" Jonas asked as Aidan came in carrying Falon.

"I'll explain everything after you check her out," Aidan said as he gently laid Falon down on the bed. "Please wake up," he begged as he brushed a piece of hair out of her eyes. After kissing her on the forehead, he moved away to allow Jonas to work.

~~~

Falon felt like she had been beat from her head to her toes. A groan slipped from her lips as pain filled her body. As she laid there she felt someone putting a cold, damp cloth to her forehead.

"Falon, are you waking up?" Aidan asked softly.

Falon slowly opened her eyes, and found Aidan looking down at her with a worried expression on his face.

"What happened?"

"Well that, my life, is a very interesting story," he said soothingly as he leaned down and kissed her softly on the lips. "However, it will wait until you have had some more rest. Are you in pain?" he asked as he watched her wince a little. If he hadn't been staring at her so intently, he wouldn't have seen it.

"A little," Falon said as she grabbed Aidan's hand and gave it a squeeze. "Don't worry so much you will get wrinkles," she joked as she tried to get Aidan to smile.

"I would be more worried about you giving me a heart attack, than me getting wrinkles from worry," he stated as he leaned over and put his forehead to hers.

"How are you feeling, Little Sis?" Jonas asked as he walked into the room. As Jonas stopped near the bed, he finally took in the scene before him. He felt like a jerk for intruding. He had been mixing some herbs and not paying attention to what was going. "Sorry, I'll leave," he said as he went to turn around and exit the room.

"No, don't leave. Falon is in pain," Aidan said as he looked over at Jonas. He watched as Jonas nodded and finished mixing the herbs.

"Here take this," Jonas said as he poured a mixture of different herbs into a cup of water.

Falon scrunched up her nose at the smell of the concoction. "That smells disgusting."

Aidan smirked at the expression his wife was making. She looked so cute with her nose scrunched up like that. Now this was his wife, straight forward and to the point. And not a flirty or flowy bone in her body.

"It may, but it will help with the pain," Jonas said as he held the cup of water up for Falon.

Falon went to sit up, but she was still too weak. She ended up just falling back against the pillow. "How long was I out?" she asked in confusion. She didn't understand why she was so weak. She closed her eyes in frustration. She must have been out for awhile if she was this weak.

Aidan saw his wife's distress and came to her aid. He gently put his arm behind her back and helped her sit up. "Eight hours."

"Then why am I so weak?" Falon asked as she took the cup, closed her eyes, and drank it as quickly as possible. When she was done, she made a face that made Aidan and Jonas both chuckle. "It tastes worse than it smells. Yuck," she exclaimed as she made another face that told them exactly how she felt about the medicine.

Aidan chuckled again then kissed Falon on the side of her head. "It may, but it will help, Love. And you're weak because Witch's Fire pushed so much power through your body while she was in you. It was the strangest thing, and I never want it to happen again."

"What?! Who?!" Falon asked loudly which she regretted when her head started pounding. "I shouldn't have gotten that loud," she said as she closed her eyes and leaned back against Aidan's arm.

"I promise, I'll explain it all later. Just rest," Aidan said as he joined her in bed and pulled her tightly to him. He watched out of the corner of his eye as Jonas quietly left the room. Aidan sighed contently as he held his wife in his arms. "You scared me. I thought I had lost you for good. And when you weren't you, I was worried that my Falon would never come back to me."

"So little faith in me," Falon said as she snuggled against her husband's chest. "I'll never fully leave you, Aidan. I'll always be with you," she said as she placed her hand over his heart and looked up into his eyes. "Always."

"Always," Aidan said as he covered her hand with his and leaned in for a kiss. It wasn't a passionate kiss, it was a gently kiss, a sweet kiss. He smiled to himself when he pulled back, and Falon was already sound asleep. "Rest, my life, and when you awaken I'll tell you everything," he said quietly as he held Falon tightly against him and closed his eyes. There would be a lot to tell her, but it would wait until she was rested. That was Aidan's last thought before he fell fast asleep with his wife in his arms.

Chapter Sixteen

"You're not going," Aidan repeated stubbornly for the fifth time. He looked over at Falon while she put her boots on. "You have just gotten back to normal."

"Yes, I am. Actually to be more specific, I'm leading the group. And I have been fine for a week, Aidan. Don't worry so much. I have done jobs like this a thousand times. We are just going to go steal some supplies, then we will be right back. No big deal," Falon said, she stood up and grabbed her cloak. After the incident with Aidan and Tomas she had gone back to changing her own clothes and had told everyone within hearing range that if anyone changed her clothes they were going to have a fight on their hands.

Aidan crossed his arms in front of his chest. "I forbid it," he ordered, his voice stern and stiff sounding.

Falon brought her head up slowly, narrowed her eyes, and glared at Aidan. "Excuse me? Did you just say you forbid me?" she asked, her voice sounding strained. Falon kept telling herself not to overreact. She needed to keep reminding herself that Aidan was just worried about her. "You forbid me?!" Falon yelled out as she put her cloak on, her eyes never looking away from Aidan's. *Well, she definitely did not remain calm.* Falon shrugged inwardly at that thought.

"Yes, I forbid you," Aidan said as he took a step closer to his wife. "You are my wife, and I won't allow you to take unnecessary risks! Especially when I'm not allowed to go with you!"

"Listen, I'm sorry that you can't come with us, but that does not mean that I'm going to stay here. I promise when I get back I'll talk to the council again," Falon said in a voice that she was happy to say was calm. She agreed that the council were being jackasses about Aidan and Cale not being able to leave, but she couldn't do anything about it right now. Well, at least they had accepted them. That was a step in the right direction. Now they just needed to get the council to agree to let them be able to leave.

One step at a time, Falon thought as she looked at her very angry and upset husband. Right now she needed to focus on what her husband was saying to her instead of what idiots the council were being. Falon looked at Aidan's jaw and saw it tense and tight. She then saw a pulse near his temple jump. Yep, she definitely needed to pay attention to her husband before he had a heart attack from being so angry.

"Falon, you're not going without me," Aidan snapped as he grabbed her by the arms and shook her.

Falon rolled her eyes and shrugged out of his hold. "You're over reacting to all of this. I went on a lot of missions before I met you, and I did just fine." *Not a good way to calm him down,* Falon thought as she saw his jaw tighten even more. How was that even possible?

"Falon, you're like a magnet for trouble!" Aidan barked as he ran his hand down his face. He couldn't let her go without him. Who would look out for her if he wasn't with her?

Oh hell no, he did not just say that, and he did not just yell at her, Falon thought as she crossed her arms in front of her chest and glared daggers at

Aidan. If looks could kill then he would be dead right now. "I'm not a magnet for trouble!" Falon shouted. "Who was the one who almost got killed in a bar? Who was the one who almost drowned?! Who was the one who was almost killed by a beast?! It sure as hell wasn't me!" Falon snapped, she got in Aidan's face.

"The bar thing was all me, but the other two were you. You were the one who pushed me off the cliff. And you were the one who I was looking for when the beast attacked me! And on top of all that you were the one who was possessed by Witch's Fire and was almost burned alive!" Aidan yelled as he put his finger in her face. He had reached his limit.

Falon scrunched her eyebrows together. "Touche." She shrugged her shoulders. "So I have had a run of bad luck, but it is not normally like this."

Aidan looked at her and brought his hand to her face, brushing his fingertips down her cheek. "I can't lose you, love." He looked at her intently begging her with his green eyes to stay.

Falon grabbed a hold of Aidan's hand, held it close to her face, and leaned in to it. "Nothing is going to happen to me. I promise."

She stepped away from Aidan and headed out of their room. As she came into the main living area, she found Cale and Ariana having a similar argument to the one her and Aidan had been having.

"Cale, I'll be fine. You need to calm your ass down and get over it," Ariana said, she grabbed her bag and headed for the main door.

"You aren't leaving without me! I almost lost you a few weeks ago. Actually, I did lose you!" Cale shouted.

"If you remember correctly, you died as well!" Ariana snapped back, she turned on her husband with what Falon assumed was supposed to be an evil expression, but it just didn't work for her. Actually, it just made everyone want to laugh when she did that face.

Falon watched the pair, and she was so involved in the stare down that she jumped when Aidan came up behind her and wrapped his arms around her waist. "See, I'm not the only one who is having difficulties with this," Aidan said as he put his chin on the top of her head and held her close with her back pressed against him.

"This is ridiculous. Cale, calm down," Falon said as she tried to move out of Aidan's arms. When she realized that she couldn't get out of his arms, she looked up at him, "Let me go, Aidan. Ariana and I have work to do."

"No, you are staying here with me," Aidan said his voice taking on the stubborn sound that he always got when he was not going to back down. In the three months they had been married, she had learned the different tones, and this was definitely the no bending one.

"What is going on here?" Jeremiah asked as he came into the room. "Falon, Ariana, you two should already be down with the others."

"We are trying, but it's not going very well," Falon said as she looked up at Aidan once again.

"I told you two not to tell them. I believe I said to tell them that you would be right back then leave."

"You what?!" Cale shouted.

Aidan's hold on Falon tightened, "We would have been worried sick not knowing where they were!"

"That is why I told you, and you see the trouble it has caused," Falon said as she motioned to his arms that were still around her waist.

Aidan sighed and put his chin back on her head, "Aidan, Cale, they will be well looked after. I promise that nothing will happen to them on this mission."

"You can't promise that," Cale said as he cut his eyes at Jeremiah. "I won't let Ariana go without me, and that's final," he said as he crossed his arms in front of his chest.

Ariana rolled her eyes and looked over at Falon. Falon gave her a raised eyebrow and Ariana knew what she had to do.

"I hope you forgive me for this one day," Falon said with a sigh.

"Forgive you for what?" Aidan asked, he looked down into Falon's eyes.

Ariana and Falon said a quick incantation under their breath, and before Aidan or Cale knew what was happening, they were knocked out and lying on the floor.

"We are going to be in so much trouble when we get back," Falon said as she made sure that Aidan hadn't hurt himself.

"Yes we are, but we had no choice. We have to go on this mission. If not then our plan can't be put into action," Ariana stated as she checked on Cale.

"Go you two. I'll keep an eye on them for you," Jeremiah said, a small smile playing at the corner of his lips. "The quicker you leave the sooner our plan can be put into action and the sooner you can come home because I'm sure that Timothy, Jonas, and I will have our hands full with them."

"I'm sure you will," Falon said with a smile then her and Ariana left the room.

~~~

"Let us out!" Aidan yelled as he stood toe to toe with one of the council members. He couldn't believe that his wife had not only knocked him out, but she had also left him. When she got home, there was going to be hell to pay.

"I can't do that," Daniel said as he tried to step back from Aidan and his anger.

"For the last three hours, you have kept me from going after *my wife!*" Aidan yelled. "What if she's hurt or captured?!"

"Others went with her. She will be fine," Daniel said as he went to walk off. "You need to stop worrying so much."

"Stop worrying! I'm not going to stop worrying about my MATE!" Aidan screamed, grabbed Daniel by the neck, and slammed him against the wall. "Let. Me. Out," he growled angrily enunciating every word as he spoke. Anger was filling him more and more as everyone tried to keep him from going after his wife.

"Aidan, put him down," Jarus said as he looked over at Aidan.

"Jarus, you and Tomas have been following me around for the last three hours, if you don't leave me alone, it is going to be you against the wall instead of him," Aidan said, neither taking his eyes off of Daniel nor loosening his grip.

"Aidan, put him down. NOW!" Falon's voice rang out throughout the entire room.

Aidan dropped Daniel instantly and turned to face off with his wife. "Where the hell have you been?!" he asked as he ran over and pulled her into his arms. He pulled her back from him and shook her. "Do you have any idea how worried I've been?!" Aidan screamed at her then he pulled her back into his arms. "You knocked me out then left me here."

"Aidan, I'm not deaf, and if you don't stop shaking me, I'm going to have neck problems," Falon said soothingly as Aidan again repeated his shaking and the pulling her close routine.

Aidan finally just pulled Falon to him and held her close. He let out a sigh of relief as she wrapped her arms around his waist and put her head against his chest, "This is where you belong. Not somewhere else."

"I know. I know," Falon said in a calm soothing voice. "So do you think my husband can go with us on missions now, or would it be safer for him to stay here?" Falon asked Daniel who was just now getting his breath back.

"I believe," Daniel said as he looked around and saw the Witches talking to Cale and Ariana and the Fae all nodding at him, "that it would be best if you are allowed to accompany Falon from now on. It would definitely be best for the ones keeping you here," Daniel said under his breath as he rubbed his throat and walked off.

Falon laughed. "Well, that went as planned," she said as she snuggled against her husband's chest.

"What are you talking about?" Aidan asked, he put his chin on top of his wife's head. He hadn't liked not knowing where she was these last three hours.

"Oh, well, we knew that the council would never let you go on missions unless you showed them how you would be if we went on one without you," Falon said with a smile as she waited for what she had just said to fully enter Aidan's head.

"You planned...but...where have you been this whole time?" Aidan asked, confusion showing in his voice.

"Outside," Falon said hesitantly. She knew that he was about to explode, and she was waiting for it.

"Outside!" Aidan yelled as he pushed away from her. "I have been going out of my mind for three hours and you were just outside!"

"Well-"

"Don't well me. It is a yes or no answer!" Aidan shouted, putting his finger in her face.

Falon wrapped her hand around his finger and gently moved it out of her face. "Yes. I was outside, but it was for a good cause," she said with a shrug. "You and Cale can now go on missions with us."

"Good cause...outside," Aidan mumbled as he ran his hand through his hair. He closed his eyes trying to get himself to calm down. Aidan thought about the torture he had been going through for the past three hours, and his anger spiked back up. "I need some time to myself,"

Aidan said as he completely moved away from Falon and walked off.

Falon let out a breath. "That could have gone a lot better."

"It could have gone a lot worse too," Ariana said as she came and stood next to her friend.

"So what did the Witches say?" Falon asked as she looked at her husband's back, watching him walk away.

"That Cale can go with me now. They believe that it would be safer for them if he went with us," Ariana chuckled. "Of course, that was before he got so angry he walked away from me."

"Yep, same with Aidan. You think they will forgive us?"

"Probably," Ariana said with a small smile. "It just may take a while."

"I'm going to go get something to eat. You want to join me?"

"May as well. I don't think Cale or Aidan will be calming down anytime soon."

"Nope, let's go eat," Falon said then the two walked off to the dining hall.

~~~

"Our wives are mean," Cale said as he leaned against the cave wall and stared out at the woods. He couldn't believe that Ariana and Falon had been here the whole time.

"No, they were trying to make it where the council would let you leave the city. Personally, I think they did you guys a favor," Jarus said as he came up behind the two. "I mean, I wouldn't want to be stuck here all the time."

"A favor? We have been worried sick about our wives, and you say it was a favor. As mad as I was I could have killed Daniel before she decided to show up," Aidan said with a glare at Jarus.

"No, she would have stopped you," Tomas said as he came over to the group. "Did you not notice that both of us would be following you then suddenly there would be only one? When

303

you did something one of us would run and tell Falon. By the time you headed for Daniel, she had already started heading in because she knew by what we were telling her that you were about to completely lose it."

"And what about me?" Cale asked, a frown marred his face. "I had no one following me."

"Timothy was. He was just better at maintaining his distance. Of the two, we were less worried about you doing something stupid. You're the calmer one," Jarus said with a shrug of the shoulders.

"So are you two going to pout all day, or go enjoy your wives before all of you get sent on a real mission?" Tomas asked with a pointed look.

Aidan looked at Cale. "I guess we will go enjoy our wives, but first, she is going to apologize to me for making me worry. Sometimes I wonder if she cares for me as much as I care for her," Aidan mumbled under his breath as he walked back towards the city.

"She does," Jarus said as he followed after Aidan.

"And how would you know?" Aidan snapped.

"Because she has never looked at someone like she looks at you, and no one has ever been allowed in her bed. And trust me there were many who tried," Tomas said with a smile towards Aidan.

"And were you two some of the ones who tried?" Aidan asked in a growl. If they said yes he was going to take them both by the throats and throw them clear across the room.

"Nope, but if you like I can point out the ones who did," Jarus said with an evil smirk.

"I don't think that is a good idea," Cale said as he shoved Aidan on the shoulder. "If the number of men are anything like the number of men who wanted to get into Ariana's bed then Aidan will be killing half the population."

Aidan shoved Cale back. "How come you aren't jealous like I am?"

"I'm jealous, but I'm also calmer than you. Besides I'm sure of Ariana's love for me," Cale

said as he looked at Aidan with a raised
eyebrow.

"Falon loves me!" Aidan snapped.

"Then there is no reason for you to be so
jealous," Tomas said with a smirk.

"I'm not used to...never mind. I'm going to
go talk to my wife instead of you three idiots,"
Aidan said as he hurried off to find Falon.

Chapter Seventeen

Falon was getting ready to leave the dining hall when she saw Aidan and Cale coming in. "Well, we're about to find out if they are still angry."

"Yes, this should be interesting," Ariana said as they started towards their husbands.

Falon was right behind Ariana until she came up behind a couple of Witches and heard what they were saying. Falon's eyes turned red, and her anger went to a new level as she listened to their conversation.

"That Fae is gorgeous," the Witch said with a sexy purr. "I can't believe he chose that whore, Falon. He probably wouldn't know what to do with a real woman."

"You could show him," the other Witch said with a sneer.

"I guess I could. If that tramp could get him in her bed then I'm sure I would have little trouble. And the things I would do to him." The Witch started to go into detail of all the things she wanted to do to Aidan.

Falon felt her fist clench at her side as she listened to the two Witches talk. No one was going to touch her husband, and no one was going to talk about him like that. Before Falon could even register what she was doing, she had come up behind the Witch that was saying all the things she was going to do to Aidan, and grabbed her by the head of the hair. Before the Witch could react, Falon had twisted her hand in the woman's hair and, with all her might, slammed the woman's face into the table. "You need to watch what you say!" Falon yelled as she jerked the woman's head back up so that the Witch was looking at her. "Aidan is mine! No one will touch him but me." She took the woman's head and slammed it into the table one more time before she was jerked away from the Witch.

Falon almost laughed when the Witch was jerked out of the chair she had been seating in because Falon's hand was still wrapped in the Witch's hair. Falon finally released her hold on the hair so she could focus on the person who was pulling her away from the tramp who dared to talk about her husband. "Let me go!" she yelled as she started to struggle against the hands trying to pull her away from the Witch on the floor.

"Falon, calm down," Aidan said against her ear. He had seen his wife start to walk towards him when he had entered the dining hall, but then she had stopped. Aidan had been confused at first, but the confusion had turned to shear panic as he watched Falon grab a woman by the head of the hair and slam her into the table. He didn't know what had happened, but he did know that as angry as Falon was she would probably do some major damage to the woman. "Calm down, love," Aidan said gently as he pulled her further away from the woman who was getting off the floor with a little help from her friends.

"Let me go, Aidan. I have a few more things I want to say to that Witch!" Falon shouted as she tried once again to get out of her husband's arms.

"No. You need to calm down before I let you go," Aidan said as he turned Falon so that she was facing him. He gripped her arms so she couldn't turn back around. "Look at me," Aidan demanded as Falon tried to wiggle out of his arms again.

Falon took a deep breath then looked up into her husband's face. "I'm calm now," she said her voice strained as she tried to reign in her anger.

Aidan looked at her red eyes and knew she was lying. "You are not calm. Now, tell me what happened," Aidan said soothingly holding her gaze. He knew something was brewing around them between the Witches and Fae, but he needed to calm Falon down before he took on anything else.

Falon didn't notice that every Fae had gathered around her and Aidan. She also didn't notice that the Witches were gathering around the woman who had talked so crass about her husband. All she knew was that Aidan wasn't going to let her go until she calmed down.

Falon closed her eyes and started taking deep breaths. She had never lost her temper like that before. Falon cringed inwardly as she thought about the fact that if Aidan hadn't of grabbed her she would have killed that Witch for what she had said about Aidan. Falon's shoulders sagged as she realized how much she had let her jealousy control her. What was wrong with her?

Aidan loosened his grip on Falon as he watched her relax. She was finally beginning to calm down. "Now, do you want to tell me why you slammed that woman's face into the table?" Aidan asked, he moved his hands up and down his wife's arms trying to sooth her with his touch.

Falon looked up at Aidan with tears in her eyes. "I could have killed her."

Aidan scrunched his eyebrows together then pulled her into his arms. "No, you would have stopped," he said as he ran his hand down her back. "Now, what happened?"

"I may have gotten a little jealous," she said as she snuggled against her husband's chest. Aidan was her's and no one was going to take him from her.

Aidan laughed. "So I guess now we know how you will handle your jealousy."

"This isn't funny," Falon said as she pulled back and looked up at Aidan. "Did I hurt her bad?"

"I don't know I haven't looked, but I do know that we are about to have a war on our hands if you don't get the Fae to back down," he said as he looked over Falon's head and saw the Fae lined up against the Witches and poor Ariana was in the middle trying to calm everyone down. "I think we should go help Ariana."

Falon turned and took in the scene around her. Her anger had consumed her so much that she hadn't thought about the consequences of her actions or even noticed the other Fae gathering around her. "This is bad. Very bad," she said nervously as she headed towards the front of the group. As Falon came closer she heard the Witch she had hit, well slammed her head into the table, calling her all kinds of names and saying that she didn't do anything to provoke Falon to such actions.

"Falon would not have attacked you unless she was provoked," Ariana shouted.

"Ariana, I think I owe this woman an apology," Falon said with great difficulty. If it wasn't for the fact that she didn't want a war to break out, then she wouldn't have apologized at all. Actually, she probably would have punched the girl in the face for good measure.

Aidan almost started laughing, but he was able to contain himself. He came up behind his wife and put his hands on her shoulders. He wanted to give her comfort and to hold onto her just in case he needed to intervene again. He didn't think he would have to, but there was no reason to take chances.

"I don't want your apology you Human trash!" the woman shouted.

Falon felt the tension the Fae were giving off double in size as the Witch got in her face and yelled at her. "You will show Falon the respect her position deserves!" Ariana said as she stepped in between Falon and the Witch, Julia. "You need to learn to hold your tongue, Julia," she said as she glared at the woman.

"She slammed my head into the table! Twice!" Julia said in a high pitched squeal, she held her fingers showing the number of times she was slammed into the table.

"My Lady, what caused you to lose your temper?" Jarus asked as he took his place next to Falon.

Falon felt every eye in the room focus their attention on her. She looked down at her fingers as she began to pick at her nails. It was something she did to keep her focus off of the fact that every eye in the room was looking at her. "I..," she sighed and cleared her throat trying to get over the embarrassment of the situation "I let my jealousy get away from me."

"Why did you become jealous of this..," Tomas stopped looked Julia up and down and with a sound of disgust said, "Witch?"

"Why the hell does it matter? She slammed Julia's face into the table. Not once but twice, and all of you Fae think that she had a good reason. There is never a good reason to behave like that. That woman," she said pointing at Falon, "is crazy!"

"Watch it, Beth," Ariana said as she took a step closer to the two women who had started this whole thing. She didn't know how, but she knew that Falon wouldn't have acted without a just cause.

"You're right. Nothing excuses me for slamming Julia's head into the table," Falon said as she leaned back against her husband. She hoped that his calmness would rub off on her because just thinking about all the things that Julia had said was enough to make her angry again. Really the girl didn't look that bad. Sure, she had a broken nose and a cut on her forehead, but it could have been worse. Falon inwardly shrugged as she took in the scene around her. There was definitely no need for all the Witches and Fae to be involved.

"Falon, what did she say?" Ariana asked as she turned and looked at her friend.

Falon looked back at her hands and began to pick at her nails once again. "I over heard her saying some things that she would like to do with my husband." When Falon said my husband her head jerked up, and her eyes met Julia's. "I didn't enjoy listening to what she was saying so I slammed her head into the table."

Falon shrugged then looked back down at her hands.

Aidan's hands tensed on Falon's shoulders as what she had just said sank in. "What exactly did she say, Falon?" he asked his voice remaining calm and steady.

Falon sighed then looked up over her shoulder at her husband. "It wasn't very nice," she said sounding very pitiful and almost childlike. Falon really had no desire to tell them all that had been said.

"Falon, we need to know," Ariana said as she looked at her friend with an apologetic look. She knew that it had to be something bad for Falon not to want to speak of it.

Falon sighed deeply then told everyone what Julia and her friend had said. She wanted to leave some things out, but she knew that if she did they would just ask more questions. By the time Falon was done speaking, her anger at returned. To get the anger to go back down, she leaned back against her husband again, and when his arms wrapped around her waist, she felt the tension begin to ease. He was hers, and he would always be with her.

Aidan wrapped his arms around Falon's waist as she leaned back against him. Personally, he thought she had handled the situation very well. If he had heard some man talking that way about Falon, he would have ripped the man's bloody head off. To him, she had showed a lot of restraint. "I love you," Aidan said as he leaned down and spoke to his wife softly. "And no one else will ever do." He then kissed her gently on the side of the neck. "Always and forever."

"If you had said that about my mate," Ariana snapped, "I would have done more than slam your head into the table," Ariana said as she took a step towards Julia and Beth. "I have half a mind to allow Falon to rip you apart, but lucky for you, I don't want to start a war between the Fae and Witches. So, you'll be stuck with me," Ariana said as she used her powers and threw both women clear across the room. Ariana then turned and looked at the other Witches. "This situation does not concern anyone else, but me and them so leave."

Falon watched as the Witches and Fae left the room very quickly. It was almost hilarious how fast the Witches left. Most of them even tripped over each other because they were in such a hurry to leave. Ariana really could be scary when she was angry enough. "Ariana, I think I did enough to them," Falon said quietly so that only Ariana would hear her.

"No, I don't think you did. What had you been planning on doing before Aidan grabbed you?" Ariana asked as she turned and looked at her friend.

Falon looked at her shoes and shuffled her feet. "I may have been thinking about sitting her hair on fire, but I think that was a bit too much."

Ariana, Cale, who had been keeping quiet the whole time, and Aidan all burst out laughing. "Yes, I believe that is a bit much. Of course, if they had been talking about Cale I would have ripped their tongues out. Well, why don't you and Aidan go, and Cale and I will deal with these two," Ariana said as she waved at the two Witches that she had pinned to the wall still.

"But..," Falon started but Aidan stopped her by pulling her away.

"Come. I have to speak with you," Aidan said as he pulled his wife away and towards their room. Once in their room, Aidan pulled Falon into his arm and kissed her with all the love and passion he felt for her.

"Wow," Falon said as Aidan pulled back and put his forehead to hers.

Aidan chuckled at her breathless response. She really was the most amazing woman he had ever met before. "Falon, you are my life, and the only woman that I have or ever will be with."

Falon started picking at the ties to his shirt, "I know."

"Do you?" Aidan asked as he grabbed her chin and made her look at him.

"Yes," Falon said with a conviction that made Aidan believe her. "And you know that you are the only one for me. Right?" Falon asked as she cupped his cheek with her hand.

Aidan leaned into Falon's hand and closed his eyes to her touch, "Yes, My Life, I know." When he opened his eyes he could see the passion in his wife's eyes. "I love you," Aidan said right before he leaned down and captured her lips with his own.

Chapter Eighteen

"We need supplies," Jeremiah said as he came over to Falon, Aidan, Cale, and Ariana.

"I guess we're up?" Falon asked as she circled her husband trying to figure out what the best point of attack was.

"Yes, it's the Fae's turn, and the council believe that you four should go. You and Ariana will be able to show Aidan and Cale the ropes. Now, be careful and don't take any unnecessary risks," Jeremiah said as he looked at his daughter.

"Why am I the only one you're looking at?" Falon asked defensively.

"Because you're the one who takes the most risks," Aidan said as he waits for Falon to attack. If she didn't attack soon he was going to fall asleep.

Taking Aidan's moment of distraction, Falon attacked. Before she even knew what had happened or how it happened, she was on her back under Aidan. "How did you do that?"

"Years of practice," Aidan said as he leaned down and kissed Falon on the nose. She was so cute when she was aggravated. "I could show you." Aidan watched as Falon tilted her head to the side, and a mischievous smile appeared on her face. That was never a good sign.

"Speaking of years, how old are you anyway?" Falon asked laughingly. If he was going to mess with her then she was going to mess with him.

"Older than you," Aidan said his smile fading as he saw the laughter in his wife's eyes. He really didn't want to talk about his age. What if he told her, and she saw him differently? Aidan went to get off of Falon, but before he could, she had rolled him onto his back.

"That is not a suitable answer," Falon said as she straddled her husband's waist and leaned forward so that her hair was curtaining his face.

"Hey you two do realize that there are other people in the room, right?" Cale asked as he leaned down and looked at the pair.

Aidan took that opportunity to shove Cale on the shoulder sending him to the floor. "No, we completely forgot that there are at least five other people in this room," he said sarcastically as he glared evilly at his friend.

"Just checking," Cale said laughingly as he got off the floor.

"Cale and I are going to go get ready. We'll be ready in three hours," Ariana said as she pushed her husband towards the door.

"But I want to stay for this conversation," Cale laughed as his wife pushed him out the door.

Aidan rolled his eyes as everyone left the room leaving him and Falon alone. Normally, he wouldn't have minded, but he really did not want to have this conversation with her. What if she found his age disturbing?

"You really don't want to tell me, do you?" Falon asked as she leaned back from him. She was about to get off him when he grabbed her by the waist holding her in place.

"I'm worried if you know it will upset you," Aidan said as he ran his hands up Falon's body.

Falon closed her eyes as her husband weaved his spell over her. "You worry too much," she said as she leaned down and captured his mouth with her own. As the kiss deepened, Aidan rolled her onto her back pinning her to the floor. He used his power to lock the doors to the room. Soon both of them forgot about anything else but losing themselves in each other's love.

~~~

"Two thousand and forty-five," Aidan said as he pulled Falon closer to him. As long as he held her close, she couldn't run away. Well, at least that was his plan.

Falon snuggled close to her husband's side. "So, you are only one thousand and twenty years older than me. Considering that technically I was born years ago. Of course, I don't remember a thousand years of it, but oh well," Falon said as she tilted her head back so she could look up at her husband's face.

Aidan was playing with Falon's hair as he looked down into her eyes. "It really doesn't bother you?" he asked a little unsure of himself.

"No, it doesn't. Do you want to know something that does bother me?" Falon asked as she put the most pitiful look on her face.

"Sure," Aidan said with a laugh. She really was his joy.

"The fact that you took me down so quickly," Falon stood up and put her clothes back on. "Oh, and the fact that we just had a moment in a common area."

Aidan laughed even harder as she shrugged her shoulders and gave him a sexy smile. "You are my joy," he said as he stood up and pulled her into his arms. "I never laughed until I met you."

"I don't know if I should be offended about that or not considering you laugh at me more than with me," Falon said with a raised eyebrow and a smirk.

"You shouldn't be offended. You should be happy that you make me happy," Aidan said right before he kissed the side of her neck.

Falon closed her eyes and wrapped her fingers in his hair as he started kissing his way to her mouth. "Aidan, we have work to do."

"Damn. I forgot about that," Aidan said as he pulled back and looked at his Falon. Yes, his Falon. She was his and she always would be.

"Come on, Love. The sooner we get this done the sooner we can get back," Falon said with a laugh as she grabbed her Aidan's hand and hurried out of the room. Her Aidan. She liked the sound of that.

~~~

"This way," Ariana said in a whisper as she pointed down a dark alley.

"Are you sure?" Falon asked her voice a little unsteady. "I know how your visions play out."

"There is nothing wrong with my visions," Ariana said defensively. Why was everyone always going on about her visions? It wasn't like anyone had ever died from them.

"Of course there isn't," Cale said as he looked at Falon pointedly and put his arms around his wife's waist.

"I have been around her longer, so I know about her visions more than you do," Falon said as she crossed her arms across her chest. "I trust Ariana with my life, but sometimes her visions have a habit of getting me hurt. Now, are we going down the dark, creepy alley, or are we going to sit here and talk?" Falon asked with a raised eyebrow.

Ariana shook her head and chuckled. "I guess my visions have been bad on your health, but they did bring you Aidan."

"Yes, they did." Aidan said as he put his arm around Falon's shoulder. "But just in case I'm going to go first."

"If you say so," Falon said as she waved him forward.

"You're not going to argue with me about this?" Aidan asked with a raised eyebrow and a skeptical look on his face.

"Nope, you go right ahead," Falon said as she leaned against the wall of the building with her legs crossed at the ankles, and her arms crossed in front of her chest. "I'll wait here. Ooh, I'll stand guard. I don't normally get to do that. Can I?" Falon asked sounding like a little child who was asking permission for something. Falon clapped her hands together and looked at Aidan with a huge smile on her face.

Aidan shook his head and chuckled. "No, you will be right behind me. Now, come on and stop stalling," Aidan said as he headed down the alley.

Falon sighed sadly then she motioned for Cale and Ariana to stay put. "Why don't I ever get to stand guard? It just isn't fair," Falon said with a pout. She kicked a stone as she walked after Aidan.

"Stop pouting. Maybe we can stand guard next time," Aidan said quietly as they continued down the alley.

"I'm not pouting," Falon said as she shuffled her feet and looked at the back of Aidan's head.

Aidan raised an eyebrow at Falon and looked over his shoulder at her. "Sure you're not," he said with a wink and a smile. She was so cute when she wasn't happy about something. She was really cute when she scrunched her nose up at him. Aidan shook his head and looked back towards where he was going.

Falon chuckled to herself as her husband looked at her. "All right, maybe I am. Come on, let's get this over with," she said as he turned back around and focused on the job.

~~~

Aidan, Falon, Ariana, and Cale came to the main door of the city laughing. "I see now why you are so hesitant about Ariana's visions," Cale said as he tried to catch his breath. Of course, as soon as he looked over at Aidan and Falon, he started laughing again. They were definitely a sight to see.

"Well, at least this time no one got injured," Ariana said as her laughter started to die down. She couldn't believe what had happened to Aidan and Falon.

"Yes, well, I think I'm going to go get cleaned up," Falon said as she looked down at herself. She was covered in mud and who knows what else.

"Yeah, I'll join you," Aidan said as they hurried off. They had completed their task, but not before him and Falon had landed in a huge pig pin. Aidan shook his head and laughed. *Life around Thief's City and around his very own little thief was never going to be boring,* Aidan thought to himself as he caught up with Falon right before they entered their room. "Do you want company?" Aidan asked with a raised eyebrow.

Falon turned and looked at her Aidan. "I would love some company," she said with a sexy smile. "Of course, we may need to take two or three baths before we get all this gunk off."

"I think I can suffer through," Aidan said with a sexy smile of his own. As they entered their room, Aidan was finally feeling like Fate was going to give them a break. They were finally going to settle into a home, and finally, they were going to have some peace.

Chapter Nineteen

"You're leaving me?!" Falon shouted as she watched her husband grab a bag and put it on his shoulder.

"I'll be back in a few days, Love," Aidan said as he went to pull Falon into his arms, but she jerked away from him. Aidan sighed deeply and ran his hands through his hair that was shorter than it had been in a long time. "Falon, it is safer for you to stay here," he said with the most pitiful face he could. Aidan didn't want to be away from her either, but the thought of her going with him and being that close to Damian did not sit well with him. He needed to keep her safe, and the way to do that was for her to stay here in Thief's City.

"What about you? You can't go into Damian's hideout without someone watching your back! No, you're not going without me. I won't let you!" Falon said panicking. She couldn't lose Aidan. She would never survive losing him, and she knew it. "I won't let you," Falon said losing some of her fire, and her voice sounding depressed. She was also sounding more like a child who wasn't getting her way, but she really didn't care right now. All she cared about was keeping Aidan with her. She didn't care how much she had to sound like a child or pitch a fit. If she had to stomp her foot to get her way then dammit, she was going to stomp her foot. Actually, she would do that right now. Falon stomped her foot and looked at Aidan with a look that said all hell was going to break loose if she didn't get her way. "You're not going unless I go too."

Aidan shook his head and took a step closer to Falon, but she countered him by taking a step back. "Falon, stop moving away from me," Aidan said through a clenched jaw. He wanted to hold her and tell her everything was going to be all right, but she was being stubborn and very childish. Aidan took another step towards his wife, but again she moved away from him. "Dammit, Falon, stop moving away from me!" Aidan shouted.

"Then don't leave me." Falon looked up into Aidan's eyes. "Don't leave me," she cried out as her voice broke.

Aidan saw the tears forming in Falon's eyes, and he felt like the biggest ass in the world. "Falon, Cale is going with me. I won't be alone, but I can't do what I need to do if I'm worrying about you. Jonathan finally gave us the information we needed. I have to go," Aidan said soothingly as he took a step towards Falon. He was shocked when she didn't move away from him, but just stood there staring at him with tears falling down her face. "Don't cry, baby. Don't cry," Aidan said as he pulled Falon into his arms and held her close. He really hated to see her like this, but there was no other way. He would not take her with him and put her in danger.

Falon put her head on Aidan's chest and let the tears fall. For some reason, she felt like if Aidan left her everything was going to fall apart. She needed to go with him. It felt wrong to stay here without him. "Please, let me go with you," Falon begged as she snuggled against his chest.

Aidan held her tight against him with one arm around her waist, and his other hand running down her hair as he tried to sooth her. "I'll be back before you know it. Falon, I need to know you're safe to be able to do my job. If I lost you, I wouldn't...I wouldn't survive." Aidan put his cheek to the top of her head and wrapped both of his arms protectively around her waist. "You are my life. You are everything to me."

Falon took a deep breath trying to get the tears to stop. "And how do you think I would feel if I lost you?" Falon asked as she wrapped her arms around Aidan's waist and snuggled against his chest. "I can't lose you."

"You won't. I'll always come back to you," Aidan said as he took her chin and tilted it up so she was looking at him. "I'll come back. I promise."

Falon closed her eyes as Aidan leaned down and kissed away her tears. "I love you more than life, Aidan. I was dead before I met you."

"I love you, and I feel the same way," Aidan whispered as his mouth came down and captured Falon's.

~~~

"Be careful, son," Jeremiah said as he gave Aidan a hug.

"I will be. Look after Falon for me," Aidan said with a lump in his throat. Jeremiah had called him son. Aidan leaned back and wrapped his arm around Falon's waist and pulled her into his side as he tried to get himself to follow through with the plan. Leaving Falon and his new family was going to be very difficult. It had been a long time since he had a family, and he really didn't want to leave them. He definitely did not like leaving his wife. His Falon.

"I will," Jeremiah said with a smile then he stepped back so Jonas could give Aidan a hug.

"I'll make sure she stays here and doesn't go after you," Jonas said with a smile as he pulled back from giving Aidan a hug.

"I would greatly appreciate it, but I believe that you'll have your hands full," Aidan said as he looked down at his wife who had yet to say anything since earlier that morning. It was really starting to worry him. He didn't like her like this. Aidan liked her fiery and full of life.

"I promised I would stay here and be good. What more do you want from me?" Falon asked her voice sounding depressed and broken.

"Falon, please don't sound like that," Aidan said as he grabbed her chin and tilted her head up so she was looking at him. He saw the tears once again begin to form in her eyes. She wasn't normally a crier so it was confusing him to see them, but it also warmed his heart. Falon loved him as much as he loved her.

"I can't help it. I just feel like something bad is going to happen if you leave me," Falon said as she jerked her chin away and tried to get her emotions under control. Falon couldn't explain what she was feeling, and honestly, it was about to drive her insane.

"Everything is going to be all right. I'll be back soon," Aidan said as he kissed her on the head. "Nothing bad is going to happen to me."

Falon sighed deeply then looked into her husband's eyes. "Be careful, and I love you."

"I love you, too," Aidan leaned down and kissed her with all the passion and love he felt.

He didn't know how long it lasted, but he knew it was long enough for Jeremiah and Jonas to start coughing to get their attention. When Aidan finally pulled back, he was having difficulties catching his breath.

Falon collapsed against her husband's chest once the kiss ended, and all she could say was, "Wow."

Aidan chuckled as he put his chin on Falon's head. "Yeah, wow."

"All right, Aidan, you need to get going," Jonas said as he looked at his sister and brother-in-law. They really were perfect for each other. Jonas felt his heart fill with pain as he looked at them. He was happy for his sister, but he was also sad that he would never have what she had. He wanted that kind of love, but he knew it would never happen.

"I know," Aidan said as he pulled back away from Falon. "I'll be back soon."

Falon nodded her head and watched as her husband walked off. She wanted to run after him and force him to stay, but she knew she couldn't. "Come back to me," she said softly to herself as Aidan disappeared out of sight.

~~~

"Where are you going?" Falon asked Ariana as she came into the room and saw Ariana putting a bag on.

"Dad needs me to go get three Witches," Ariana said as she came over to Falon and hugged her, "It won't take very long. I should only be gone for a day at the most."

"I'll go with you. Aidan and Cale have been gone for three days, and I need time away from here," Falon said as she left the room and headed for her own. Something in her was telling her she needed to leave. Falon couldn't explain the feeling, she just knew that she wasn't supposed to be here.

"Falon, you can't go on this mission with me. The three Witches I'm going after are skittish enough. Dad only wanted me to go after them. Besides, you promised Aidan you would stay here, and Jonas is not going to let you leave."

Falon rubbed her face with her hand, "I know what I promised, but something in me is telling me I need to leave. I don't know what's going on, but I know I'm not supposed to stay here."

"Falon, nothing is going to happen here. I'll be back soon."

"Why does everyone keep saying that to me? I'm not crazy!" Falon yelled as she ran her hand through her hair in frustration. "Will you at least try to look into the future and tell me what you see?" Falon asked as she grabbed Ariana by the arm stopping her from leaving.

Ariana sighed. "You are not the only one whose husband left, you know?"

"I know, Ariana, and I'm sorry, but I need you to look. Please," Falon pleaded as she looked at her friend.

"I'll try," Ariana said as she closed her eyes and tried to get a glimpse of the future. She looked and looked, but nothing stood out. She could see nothing. "I'm sorry, Falon. Listen, when I get back maybe I can talk Jonas into letting you leave for a short time. Maybe that will help with this restlessness you are feeling," Ariana said as she hugged her friend then walked off.

Falon watched as her friend left. "It isn't restlessness. It's foreboding," Falon said to herself as Ariana left the city. Falon pinched the bridge of her nose and hoped that what she was feeling was just the fact that Aidan was gone, and not because something bad was going to happen.

~~~

Aidan looked around the dark alley as he waited for Cale. They had been gone for three days, and he was ready to get home to Falon. He knew that Cale was just as anxious to get back to Ariana, so he wasn't going to be snappy because Cale was late. Aidan let out the breath he didn't know he had been holding when Cale appeared in the alley. "You're late," Aidan said smoothly.

"Yeah, sorry. You ready to get out of this damn place?"

"Yes, I'm ready to get back to my wife," Aidan said as they hurried through the alley.

"Me too. I could do with a little light in my life. These past few days have been filled with nothing but darkness," Cale said as they came to the end of the dark alley.

"I know what you mean. Come on if we hurry we can be there by nightfall tomorrow," Aidan said as he led the way out of the city that Damian had made his home. Aidan felt a shiver go down his spine as he thought about his so called father. Damian had gotten even worse than he had been the last time Aidan had seen him. Damian was so filled with lust for power that he was going against every Fae law that had been written. Aidan knew that there was going to come a time when he would have to fight Damian and end his reign of terror. When they had killed the Elementals, Aidan had thought that they would have peace, but now, he knew that they would never have peace as long as Damian ruled the Fae. It was time for a change. Aidan shook his head to get his thoughts away from things that were so dark, and he focused on Falon. His life and light in the darkness. With her by his side, he knew that no matter what challenges came his way he would be fine. As long as he had Falon, nothing could stop him.

~~~

Falon woke up suddenly as she heard an explosion go off. She hurried out of her bed, got dressed, and ran out of her room without even bothering to put her shoes on. As she ran out of her room and towards the explosion there was utter chaos. Witches and Fae were trying to protect the Humans from the explosions that were going off. Falon hurried over to a couple of Humans and put a shield up as a flaming piece of rock huddled its way towards them.

"Go!" she yelled as she destroyed the rock. A sense of dread fell over Falon as she watched Damian's Fae army break through the gates of Thief's City.

She ran towards the head of the group to the few Fae and Witches that actually knew how to fight. Most of the ones living in the city were just thieves nothing more.

Out of the three hundred and thirteen people living in Thief's City there were only a little over thirty of them that actually knew how to fight. Falon knew against the Fae that were pouring in they were not going to stand a chance.

She took her place in between her father and Jonas. "This is going to be a long day," Falon said as she put up a shield to keep Damian's army at bay for just a little while longer. "If I keep the shield up, can you get everyone out?" Falon asked as she strained against all the power that was being thrown at her shield. They were in deep trouble this time.

"You won't be able to hold it that long," Jonas said as he put his hand on her shoulder. "We are going to have to fight."

Jeremiah looked at his children with a serious look on his face, "I'm sorry. I should have protected you two better."

"Dad, you couldn't have foreseen this. Besides, I would rather us all go out together if that is what is going to happen anyway," Jonas said as he looked at his father.

Falon looked at her family, and she smiled sadly when her father and Jonas' eyes met hers. "Let's give them hell," she said so loud that the Fae and Witch guards all heard her. They all cheered and got ready for her shield to fall. Falon took a deep breath, and with a push of her hands, she threw her shield at the Fae knocking about half of them down. For at least a few minutes, they would have the advantage. Falon pulled her power, every bit she had and started attacking. Out of the corner of her eye, she saw her family fighting with everything they had in them.

Falon was so worried about everyone else that she didn't notice when a Fae came up behind her. She was fighting a Fae in front of her when she suddenly heard her father yell. A dread filled her like she had never felt before as she killed the Fae she was fighting and turned in time to catch her father as he fell to the ground. Falon watched as Jonas killed the Fae that had tried to kill her from behind. If her father wouldn't have stepped in between her and the Fae, she would be dead now. "Dad? Dad!" Falon said as she braced his head in her arms.

"Go. Fight," Jeremiah said as he looked up at his daughter. "You. Have. To live. For Aidan." Jeremiah took a breath and started coughing.

"I can't leave you," Falon said as tears fell down her face. She touched his face with her hand then looked up to see Jonas kneeling next to her.

"Come, Little Sister, we have a war to fight," Jonas said as he stood up and pulled Falon away from their father. "There is nothing we can do for him," he said as tears slid down his face.

Falon wiped her tears away and let her anger take control. "To the end," she said as she looked at her brother.

Jonas saw the fire in her eyes, and he nodded his approval. "To the end, my little fire bug," he said with a sad smile.

Falon nodded, and the two joined the fight once again. Both of them knew that they would probably not come out of this fight alive, but they would take out as many Fae as possible before they died.

~~~

"We will be back home in about three hours," Cale said as he looked over at his friend.

"Cale, did you find it odd that most of Damian's men were not at the hideout?" Aidan asked as he stepped over a log. Something about the whole situation was bothering him. The fact that Damian and about half of his men were gone, and that he couldn't get over the feeling that something was wrong back home was making him uneasy. He didn't know why, but he had a feeling that Falon wasn't safe. It had been bothering him for about two hours now. Aidan shook his head knowing that Thief's City was the safest place for his wife. He was just being paranoid. Falon was fine. She was safe. She had to be.

"They were probably out causing trouble like normal. Listen, we know for a fact that place was the right hideout. We'll worry about where they all went later. Right now, let's just get home," Cale said as he patted his friend on the back.

"Agreed," Aidan said as he hurried along. He needed to get home.

~ ~ ~

Falon was tired, and she didn't know how much longer she could continue to fight. They had been fighting for what seemed like hours, and it didn't even seem like they had made a dent in Damian's army. Falon looked around her, and a scream escaped her as Timothy went down. He was the last of the Witches. Falon felt like a weight had settled in her gut as she looked around and noticed that only Jarus, Tomas, Jonas, and herself still fought. Falon hurried over to the three that were left, and together they put up a shield holding the Fae back. "We won't be able to keep this shield up for long," Falon said as she put her hands on her knees and tried to calm down her breathing.

"No, we won't," Jonas said as he pulled Falon into a hug. "Until the end," he said as he pulled back and looked into her eyes.

Falon nodded as a tear escaped from her eye. "Until the end."

"It has been an honor serving with you, My Lady," Jarus said as he hugged her.

"Same, Jarus." Falon said as she moved away from him and hugged Tomas, "We always did get ourselves into hopeless situations."

"Yes, but we always found a way out," Tomas said as he pulled back and looked at her sadly. "I'm afraid that this time there is no way out."

Falon nodded. "No, we will fight until the end, and we will die with honor," Falon said bravely, but inside, she was screaming at Fate. She would never see Aidan again. She would never get to hold him or tell him she loved him again. Falon closed her eyes, and for once, thanked Fate. At least, she would die knowing that Cale and Ariana were both safe and would have a chance at the happiness that her Aidan would never know. Falon opened her eyes and looked at the Fae that were fighting against them. They were almost through the shield, it would only be a matter of seconds before the broke through completely. Falon took a deep breath. "I love you, Aidan and I'll always be with you," Falon said softly as the shield broke, and the Fae rushed them.

~~~

"Did you hear that?" Aidan asked as he stopped and looked around him.

"No, what did you hear?" Cale asked as he looked at his friend in confusion.

"I could have sworn I heard Falon," Aidan rubbed the back of his neck as he closed his eyes and replayed what he had thought she said.

"What was it exactly that she said? Hurry up," Cale laughed.

"No," Aidan said seriously. "She said I love you, and I'll always be with you. She sounded like she was-" Aidan stopped as he thought about how exactly she sounded. To be honest, she sounded like she was in a battle, and she was about to lose. The sadness in her voice was unlike anything he had ever heard from her. "We need to get home. Now!" Aidan yelled as he took off running for home. Something was horribly wrong.

~~~

Falon turned around just as a Fae cornered Teresa and her baby Chloe. Without any thought, she ran towards her Human friends.

As she neared, the Fae that was about to kill her friends, he turned to see her coming towards him.

Falon pulled some power and threw it at the Fae's head. The Fae shielded himself from the first shot, but from the second he was not able to. She came over to Teresa just in time to step in front of her as two more Fae came at them.

Falon didn't even have time to put a shield up as the blast hit her in the chest knocking her back. She felt like she was on fire as her lungs struggled to breath. She felt numb as she watched the two Fae kill Teresa and baby Chloe. Falon felt tears falling down her face, but she was unable to do anything about them or the destruction that was going on around her.

Falon watched as James and the other children were killed as they tried to make their way to Teresa and Chloe. She felt like her heart was being ripped out of her chest as one by one all of the people, who had thought they were safe in Thief's City, were killed without mercy.

Falon tried to turn her head, but she couldn't. The only things she seemed to be capable of moving were her eyes, and she moved them everywhere, taking in everything. As Falon looked around her eyes feel on Jarus, Tomas, and Jonas. All three of them were trying to get to her. Falon watched as Jarus killed one Fae and turned. Their eyes met, but then she watched as Jarus fell to the ground.

Falon tried to move. She wanted to kill the Fae who had killed her friend. If Jarus had been focusing on fighting instead of trying to get to her he would still be alive, but for how much longer.

She turned her eyes to Tomas and watched as he hurried over to her. He was almost to her when a Fae shot a bolt of power at his back causing him to fall to the ground. Falon closed her eyes as yet another friend died because of her. If she had only been stronger, more able to use her Elemental powers then maybe this would have all ended differently. Falon opened her eyes looking for the last remaining fighter. Jonas. She watched as her brother sent two Fae flying, but then he turned towards her. She wanted to call out for him to stay focused, but she couldn't. She couldn't say anything. With her heart breaking in two, she watched as her brother, her best friend, fell to the ground unmoving.

Anger filled her like never before, but still she couldn't move. She closed her eyes waiting for death to take her. Hoping it would come soon, so she would no longer have to listen to the screams of the Humans, Witches, and Fae who were being slaughtered. Her friends, family, were all being wiped out. Men, women, children. All were being murdered. Falon wanted to cover her ears to stop the torture of listening to those she had come to care about die, but she couldn't. This was worse than any torture Damian could have ever done to her. Listening and watching everyone die, and not being able to do anything about it was worse than anything Damian had ever done or could ever do to her. This was pure hell. Falon opened her eyes as she heard a voice that she recognized and hated coming towards her. She moved her eyes up and met the eyes of Damian.

"Well, well. If it isn't my little Elemental," Damian said as he knelt down beside Falon.

Falon glared at him with all the hatred and anger she was feeling, but she couldn't do or say anything.

"You're well on your way to dying, but I can't allow that. It doesn't work for my plans, you see. I have a lot of things I plan for us to do together," he said as he brushed a piece of hair out of her face.

Falon felt like she was going to be sick as the monster touched her.

"Bring her," Damian yelled as he stood up and looked behind him.

Falon closed her eyes and focused on the one hope she still had. Aidan. *I'm sorry, Aidan* she thought as Damian's guard picked her up. The sudden movement sent pain throughout her body causing her mind to drift into darkness.

Chapter Twenty

Aidan ran with all his might trying to get back home as soon as possible. As he neared one of the entrances to the city, he saw Ariana coming from the opposite direction with three female Witches following close behind her.

"You're in a hurry," Ariana said with a smile on her face which quickly faded when she saw the distressed look on Aidan's face. "What's wrong?"

"Falon?" is all Aidan asked as he tried to catch his breath.

"She's inside. I'm sure in bed. What is going on?" Ariana asked as a panic started to take control of her.

Aidan shook his head and took off running inside. Something was wrong, he could feel it. As Aidan hurried through the tunnels, the smell of smoke and death hit him like a slap in the face causing him to stop in his tracks. "Do you smell that?"

"Yes," Cale said nervously as he pulled some power. "Ariana, stay behind me."

"Like hell," Ariana said as she took off running towards her home.

"Ariana!" Cale yelled out as he took off after his wife and the three Witches that were with her.

Aidan finally was pulled out of the shock. He shook his head and took off running again. He hurried through the tunnel, but he came to a dead stop when he noticed that Cale, Ariana, and the three Witches were standing in the doorway staring at something.

"What's wrong?" Aidan asked breathlessly as he pushed his way in between them. He felt his breath catch in his throat, and his heart stop as he saw all the destruction before him. "Falon?" he said his voice breaking as he looked around at the bodies that littered the ground.

"Falon!" Aidan screamed as he hurried down the stairs to the main floor. Panic filled him as he started looking at all the bodies. "Falon!" he screamed again as he continued to look for his wife.

"Please don't let her be here. Please don't let her be dead," Aidan pleaded out loud to himself as he continued to look around frantically. As he looked around he saw that Ariana, Cale, and the three other Witches were searching through the people as well. So far it looked like they hadn't found Falon. Of course, they hadn't found anyone alive either.

Every body Aidan came to was lifeless. He looked at yet another body, and he fell to his knees as he saw that it was Jeremiah.

"Jeremiah," Aidan said softly as he touched the man's chest. He was shocked to feel it rise and fall. "Jeremiah," he said as he lifted the man's head up and propped it up with his own arm. "Just hang on. I'll get Cale and you'll be all right," Aidan said as he looked down at the man who had become more like his father than his own father had ever been. He couldn't let Jeremiah die.

"Aidan," Jeremiah rasped out. He knew he didn't have much time, but he knew he had enough time to tell Aidan about Falon.

"Don't talk. Cale is going to fix you right up," Aidan said as he looked around for Cale. He was about to motion for Cale to come over when Jeremiah grabbed his hand.

"Not going to help. I need to tell you about Falon," Jeremiah said with difficulty. "You have to get her back," he gasped out.

Aidan jerked his head back towards Jeremiah. "Where is she? Where's Falon?" Aidan asked, his voice growing panicky.

"Damian," was all Jeremiah got out before he breathed his last breath.

Aidan used his hand to close Jeremiah's lifeless eyes. "I'll get her back. I promise," he vowed as he slowly lowered Jeremiah back to the ground.

When Aidan looked back up he saw Cale and Ariana around Timothy. Anger filled him as his eyes fell on all the destruction around him. Damian had done this. He had destroyed everything and everyone without mercy.

Aidan stood up with his fists clenched at his side. Damian had his Falon and nothing was going to stop him from getting her back.

To be continued...

COMING SOON!

THE FIRE TRILOGY

Witch's Fire

J. L. HACKETT